Adrianne Geffel

ALSO BY DAVID HAJDU

Love for Sale:
Pop Music in America

Heroes and Villains:
Essays on Music, Movies, Comics, and Culture

The Ten-Cent Plague:
The Great Comic-Book Scare and How It Changed America

Positively 4th Street:
The Lives and Times of Joan Baez, Bob Dylan,
Mimi Baez Fariña, and Richard Fariña

Lush Life:
A Biography of Billy Strayhorn

Adrianne Geffel

A Fiction

DAVID HAJDU

W. W. NORTON & COMPANY
Independent Publishers Since 1923

Adrianne Geffel is a work of fiction. All incidents and dialogue, and all characters, with the exception of some well-known historical and public figures, are products of the author's imagination and are not to be construed as real. Where real-life historical or public figures appear, such appearances are invented and do not change the entirely fictional nature of the work. In all other respects, any resemblance to persons living or dead is entirely coincidental.

Printed in the United States of America
First Edition

For information about permission to reproduce selections from this book, write to Permissions, W. W. Norton & Company, Inc., 500 Fifth Avenue, New York, NY 10110

For information about special discounts for bulk purchases, please contact W. W. Norton Special Sales at specialsales@wwnorton.com or 800-233-4830

Manufacturing by Lake Book Manufacturing
Book design by Daniel Lagin
Production manager: Lauren Abbate

Library of Congress Cataloging-in-Publication Data

Names: Hajdu, David, author.
Title: Adrianne Geffel : a fiction / David Hajdu.
Description: First edition. | New York, NY : W. W. Norton & Company, [2020]
Identifiers: LCCN 2020008287 | ISBN 9780393634228 (hardcover) |
ISBN 9780393634235 (epub)
Subjects: LCSH: Musicians—Fiction.
Classification: LCC PS3608.A545356 A65 2020 | DDC 813/.6—dc23
LC record available at https://lccn.loc.gov/2020008287

W. W. Norton & Company, Inc., 500 Fifth Avenue, New York, N.Y. 10110
www.wwnorton.com

W. W. Norton & Company Ltd., 15 Carlisle Street, London W1D 3BS

1 2 3 4 5 6 7 8 9 0

For Renee Rosnes and Fred Hersch,
who play with true feeling

Nothing after this page is true.

CONTENTS

INTRODUCTION

The *Oxford English Dictionary* tells us this much:

> **gef·fel** \ˊgəf·əl\ *v* (1987) **geffels, geffelled, geffelling** 1 a: to release pure emotion in a work of creative expression, esp. music, with no filter, restraint, or regard for the effect on others: *geffel on, geffel through, geffel along.* BLURT, EGEST b.: to risk hurting another in order to be true to one's self 2 a: *vi* **gef·felled** to have experienced exposure to unfiltered emotion in an artwork, whether for pleasure or educational purpose, out of perverse impulse, or to win a wager: *totally geffelled, geffelled to death.* **ˊgef·fel·ly, ˊgef·fel·ˊesque** *adj* **ˊgef·fel·ˊesque·ly** *adv* [Orig. Adrianne Geffel, Am. musician]

Like most people, I suppose, I knew what the word "geffel" meant before I knew much about the idiosyncratic American pianist and composer whose music inspired the term. My college friend Colleen broke up with her boyfriend for "geffelling" her one too many times. When Colleen and I started dating, in an ill-considered rebound experiment, things collapsed in a squabble over which of the two of us was "only geffelling," "over-geffelling," or "not geffelling enough." At one of the first publications I wrote for, a now-defunct alt-weekly in Boston, *The Real Paper*, an editor called for sizable revisions in an early piece of mine, scrawling in the margins, "GIMME SOME GEFFEL!" Try as I would, I could never fully satisfy that request. In similitude, as in reality, only one person could deliver what the subject of this book gave the world.

I had a vague grasp of the fact that a real human being named Adrianne Geffel did something so unique and important that her name had fallen into common usage. There are nods to the woman behind the word in many of the ways people evoke her sensibility. I can hardly imagine an election cycle without political commentators flinging her name in both praise and rebuke, lauding one candidate's fiery rhetoric as "Geffel-worthy," and decrying another's lack of message discipline as "going full Geffel." A living (or, some suspect, once-living) person with the name Adrianne Geffel peeps through the buzzy crosstalk.

In time, I began to discover what it was about Adrianne Geffel that led her to enter the *lingua franca* of American culture. I gave her music a listen and was hit hard by the elemental truth of her work: No one has ever made music like the music of Adrianne Geffel. Put plainly, with no hyperbole, her music is not to be believed.

How was it possible for any mere human to create work so powerful, so disruptively unshakable? Who *was* the artist who created such an art? I needed to know and set out to learn all I could about Adrianne Geffel. I found the path to that knowledge a bumpy one.

At this point in our cultural history, Adrianne Geffel is surely name-checked and referenced more freely than understood deeply. Most of what we think we know about Adrianne Geffel—and much of what we know we think about her, and some of what we know we know—is received knowledge and may be somewhat questionable, based not on the facts of her life and work but, rather, on the many ways Geffel and her music have been portrayed in popular culture, represented and appropriated over the years.

For instance, how literally should we take Sofia Coppola's Oscar™-nominated *Geyser*, a semi-factual, semi-fictional film "inspired by" the life of Adrianne Geffel? It's obvious that we are meant to see Geffel in the character of pianist/psych patient Darian (no last name mentioned in the film, though we can see in one brief shot in the scene of her rifling through her wallet for money to pay her hypnotist that the surname on her driver's license is McGuffel). Are we intended then to believe that the real-life Adrianne Geffel, like Darian in the film, administered self-shock treatments with a rewired hair curler?

In the realm of literature, much the same, Geffel was clearly the model for the pivotal character—a musically gifted alien being from a frozen, dying, Syracuse-like other dimension—in George Saunders' short story "The Girl with the Headphone Head." Yet this should hardly be taken as a suggestion that Adrianne Geffel is or was ever an actual alien.

Images of Adrianne Geffel, enigmatic and inescapable, waft through American culture to remind us of her inescapability as an enigma. The fine-art world paid prominent homage to her when the new Whitney Museum opened with the show "Impulse and Impetus: (Re)Imagining Adrianne Geffel." In the varied spheres of music, Geffel has been cited as an influence on artists as popular as Cardi B, who paid vivid tribute to her in the number-three pop hit "Bite My Tits":

You can bite my tits
For a nickel
Make it hurt
Like Adrianne Geffel

Through all of this, Adrianne Geffel is simultaneously ever-present and ever-elusive—as an abstraction, ubiquitous, and as a person, the opposite.

This book is an attempt—dare I say the first attempt I know of, if not the first attempt of my own—to tell the full story of Adrianne Geffel's life and music. Two previous books have taken up the subject of Geffel from narrower points of view, of course.

My Adry: Biran Zervakis Tells the Intimate, Inside Story of His Discovery, Adrianne Geffel by Biran Zervakis as Told to Dominic Palazzo and Isabel Weinstein-Palazzo, out of print since its publication, attracted some attention before it was withdrawn from distribution over charges of plagiarism from the estate of Sidney Sheldon. A somewhat technical study of Geffel's medical history has also been published as *She Heard Music but There Was No Instrument There: How America's Top Neurologist Changed Adrianne Geffel's Life* by Dr. Emil Vanderlinde. It is of specialized interest but not without value to readers with the necessary scientific training and curiosity about the author.

My goal in researching and writing this book was to construct as full and evocative a portrait of Adrianne Geffel as possible through the testimony of those who knew Geffel best, knew her fairly well, or knew her somewhat better than that, as well as those who just knew her. I made every effort to find and interview as many firsthand witnesses to Geffel's life who were still living at the time of my inquiry and willing to speak forthrightly, without bias, and cede the copyright to their comments. All interviews were conducted in person, typically in the interviewees' homes, assisted-living quarters, or workplaces, at the Panera Bread in Quakertown, Pennsylvania, or alongside my faculty cubicle at Columbia University, over a period of more than nine years, but less than ten, beginning in the summer of 2009. I retained all the interview testimony for use in this book by means of memory or a Tascam DR-05 portable digital audio recorder.

In duty to the principles of oral history, I strove to trigger memory and facilitate reflection, and sought not to distort through the questions I posed or the manner I have presented the answers in these pages, notwithstanding necessary alterations to avoid reader confusion or legal action. To maintain the appropriate focus on the interview content, I have not included my questions to the interviewees, unless they are necessary for space-filling or comprehension. I edited primarily for sense and grammar, augmenting the recorded interview testimony with my own language and/or ideas only when the interviewees proved disappointing.

Over the course of this work, I have come to admire Adrianne Geffel far more than I did before I learned anything about her. While I never had the good fortune to meet her or see her perform, I feel, through the candor and richness of the lessons those I've interviewed have taught me, that I almost know Adrianne Geffel—and not just as a word, a concept, or a historical figure, but as the subject of this book.

CHAPTER 1

Favorite Corners

(1959–1968)

Carolyn Geffel (mother):

Before we realized there was something wrong with her, we thought Adry was just the happiest little girl in town. She never cried, not very much at first. She needed for nothing but her bottle when it was feeding time. Both of our children were bottle babies, so you know. Adrianne was born in the year of 1959—on May 19, 1959, to give you the exact date—and our son Donny, for Donald, preceded her by three years, a few months, and I don't remember how many days, exactly. You'd have to do that arithmetic.

We gave her the name of Adrianne: A-D-R-I-A-N, plus another N and an E. Her full, official name was—I should say *is*, because that's the way I feel on the subject—her name *is* Adrianne Antoinette Geffel. We just loved the name Adrianne. It has nothing to do with Rocky's girlfriend or the Anti-Christ. They both came along after we named our Adrianne. I'm not talking about the *real* Anti-Christ. I don't know much about that. We're not very religious. My husband Greg and I just enjoyed the sound of the name: "Adrianne"—you could emphasize the last syllable, if you wanted to, and it would sound a little French. Adri-*anne—tre* continental. "*Bon jour, Adrianne! Como tale vu?*"

I took French in high school, instead of Spanish or German, and I would have continued with the language if I had gone to college, which I had definitely planned to do. I was accepted to Cedar Crest College in Allentown with a partial scholarship for accounting, but that wasn't in the cards once our first child, Donny, came along and Greg and I fell in love and got married. So it's "Adrianne," and most people pronounce it like the boy's name, Adrian, and that, in fact, is how Adry always pronounced it or pronounces it, probably, to this day.

I'm sorry my French is so rusty. There's German on Greg's side of the family. They call it Pennsylvania Dutch here, but a lot of people know it's really German. So I've picked up some of the German language from Greg's older aunts and uncles, when we saw them on the holidays and funerals. I have no prejudice against the German people or their language. I just didn't want to name my daughter Olga, so we named her Adrianne.

Gregory Geffel (father):

As my wife Carolyn has stated correctly, both Don and Adrianne were nourished on baby formula in the period of their infancy.

We recognized that option as both nutritionally beneficial and more sanitary. Hell, it *is* a formula. It is developed by scientists of baby nutrition. Also—a secondary consideration for us as parents, we received a good discount on formula, through our business associations with the A&P as the primary propane distributor for the county. The A&P does not merchandise propane on the retail level. However, it utilizes a fair amount of canister fuel in the making of prepared foods, and while that was a fairly new grocery category in that time period, it did call for the use of propane.

Carolyn Geffel:

Looking back, now that we know what Greg and I know about Adry and her condition, I do wonder if she might not have been better off on breast milk, rather than the bottle. Something funny could very well have slipped into the formula at the factory. There would be no way for us to know if some foreign something-or-other got mixed up with the formula. Some trace amounts of Clorox or VO5 or anything like that could have gotten into one of the baby bottles, and we'd never know.

Gregory Geffel:

One thing you need to understand is there's no such thing as one hundred percent purity. The government even allows for this. Regulators factor this into the regulations. If what you're buying is liquid propane, and that's what you're paying for, the law takes into account that life is not perfect. That tank of what you're purchasing on the assumption that you're getting propane might be just ninety-six, ninety-seven percent pure, and that is legally permissible. I don't understand all the intricacies of baby formula as well as I know household fuel, but I know nothing is a hundred percent.

Carolyn Geffel:

Well, our baby Adry was the closest thing to perfect I ever saw, as long as there was no music playing.

I can still picture her sitting in her playpen. She would stay there for hours and never even look at her toys. I had an adorable stuffed koala bear in a polka-dot dress when I was a girl, and I kept it my whole life to pass on to a girl of my own, when I was lucky enough to have one, and I gave it to Adry. The poor dress had disintegrated by that point, but the little bear survived. I called her Koalie—I guess that may not seem very imaginative, but that was her name. Adry'd be there in her playpen with Koalie, and they would sit there together, perfectly quiet and still, like two pretty little toys. It was so sweet to see. She had baby dolls in precious little baby-doll outfits and stuffies and all the usual rattles and balls and blocks with the letters of the alphabet on them. She wanted for nothing, and that's all she wanted in the world—nothing.

Once she started crawling, she would scoot around the floor and find her way to a corner of the room, and sit there for hours.

She had her favorite corners, like everyone. She favored the far corner in the living room, down by the door to the bathroom. I could keep an eye on her well enough from where the couch and the chairs were, if I kind of got halfway up from my seat and looked down there. She liked to sit there in her favorite corner and just hum little tunes.

Donald Geffel (brother):

There are some pictures in the picture boxes of Adry and me in our room before they made her her own room. Have you seen them? They're before anything I actually remember. I was only three or four. I know there's one of me standing on my bed. I'm dressed up in my Zorro P.J.'s and acting like I'm Zorro. I haven't seen it in a while. We got all the old pictures out when Adry got famous. The writers liked to run photos to show her before she became the well-known Adrianne Geffel. My parents gave me some of the old Kodak snapshots they dug up, but I think they kept that one, and now all that stuff is packed away. My uncle Bobber has a lot of it. It would be fun to dig it out again, now that she's not around.

I had a cool toy rifle, and I'm posing with it in that picture, pretending it's a sword. I was pretty creative like that, although Adry inevitably got more credit in the creativity department. It looked like I was pointing the sword at Adry—it was a rifle, but in my imagination, it was a sword. You could see her there in the picture, I'm pretty sure, sitting in the corner humming one of her little songs. I doubt very much that I was actually pointing at her, really. I don't recall playing with her very much. She kept to herself, and so, so did I.

I had to be four or five when they did the construction and moved the propane gear into the garage, or what used to be the garage, and Adry and I got rooms of our own. It was around the time I started kindergarten, because they knew I was going to school and, owing to the fact of Adry's activities, they wanted to get the propane tanks away from us.

Gregory Geffel:

Carolyn had been observing Adrianne's behavior and growing concerned. The both of us were concerned. Carolyn conjectured the possibility that propane might be leaking from the tanks we kept in inventory in a storage space adjacent to the kids' bedroom. Consequently, I converted our garage into a storage facility and made the original storage space into a bedroom for Adrianne. From that point forward, we parked the car on the street in front of the house. As you can imagine, that added to my workload in the winter months. Out in our part of Pennsylvania . . . we're not fifty miles from the Canadian border, one hour from Ohio, driving west on Route 80 and not much longer to Lake Erie and after that, to Canada, going north. There's no interstate north/south here, so the road time on the state highway is slower.

Carolyn Geffel:

She positively cooed in tune—little melodies, like nursery rhymes and lullabies, only not any ones we sang to her. She made them up herself in her own head and sang them to herself. I don't mean singing with words, because she wasn't really making words yet, and she was making music—sweet little tunes that she would hum to amuse herself.

[Geffel is asked if all the music her daughter made could be described as "sweet."]

Oh, that's a point to consider, yes. She made all kinds of music, you could say—happy and sad, quiet and sometimes just terribly boisterous—depended on her mood. If she was colicky, she could make some awfully colicky sounds. Fortunately, Adry was mostly a very happy little girl.

Donald Geffel:

I was only in kindergarten when I realized for the first time how things were different with Adry as my sister. We were playing Play-Doh. I was very good at Play-Doh. Remember, I told you, I had a distinct creative streak. I was working hard on my project and must have started humming to myself. The teacher said, "Donny, what a pretty tune you're humming! What song is that?"

I said, "Oh, that? That's something my baby sister made up. She sings it to herself."

The teacher said, "Well, your sister learned herself a very pretty song."

I said, "She didn't learn it. She made it up. She makes up her own music and sings it to herself all day. It's kind of annoying."

And the teacher said, "You're very clever, Donny. But it's not nice to fib. Don't be a fibber. Good boys don't fib."

I smooshed my Play-Doh into a clump and brought it home from school and told my mother, "Look—I made a present for Adry."

Gregory Geffel:

You may be aware of historical accounts of the way Einstein could do mathematics before he could talk. Ted Williams could run before he could walk. I cannot personally verify those particular things—I never had the opportunity to meet Einstein or Ted Williams when they were infants. I never knew either of them at any age. Yet, I did have the opportunity to know my daughter. I heard her humming beautiful music before she spoke a word of English. Some individuals might contend that some of it was not beautiful, per se. Yet, it was music to my ears, because it was music made by my daughter, and I heard it with my own ears.

Both my wife Carolyn and myself were surprised by Adrianne's reaction to her music, at the juncture when she had the opportunity to hear it for herself. My brother Bobber—you should put his name down as Robert, to have it legally—Bobber gave us some assistance in this regard in 1961 or '62—Adry was approximately two years of age. Bobber was in the sales field, in wholesale fabric. He was the Romeo in the family. Still is. At this point in time, he was recently divorced from his first wife, Rosemary—divorced or legally separated. It was legal for him to be dating at this point, finally. As you can imagine, he had the opportunity to meet quite a few women in the fabric industry—designers and so forth. He was keeping company with a young lady who was known to have a roommate—or a sister or a cousin, I can't be held to all the fine points of this—and the roommate or sister or what-have-you worked in the business office of the county hospital. They had a tape recorder in the hospital, for some reason. I suppose they had a recording of last rites that they could play if a patient wasn't going to make it and a priest couldn't get there in time. My brother was very resourceful, which did get him in some trouble with his wives. This time, it was all for the good. He arranged to borrow the tape recorder and lugged it to our house so we could record Adry humming one of her songs. Bobber told me we could keep the tape recorder if we would like, but it didn't quite work out to record Adry, and we returned the machine to him. I suspect he still has it, if you're interested to see it. It was a Grundig, portable but could also work through the household AC current. It came from Germany, like my family.

Carolyn and Bobber and I—and, I believe, Bobber's girlfriend, who became his second wife—set it up on the floor of the living room, in the far corner Adry used to enjoy. Adry took a look at it and inched back against the wall and stared at it. Bobber turned it on, and the tape reels started to spin. Adry was fascinated by that—you know how kids like gadgets, especially when they have a pair of spinning reels on top? I got quite a charge out of it myself. Adry studied it and started to hum a happy song. We got it on tape, and Bobber pressed the STOP button when she stopped. The tape is still with Bobber, in a whole collection of things from Adry's very early days of making music that Bobber organized for safekeeping.

The trouble began when we played the tape back through the recorder. As soon as Adrianne heard that, she started to cry. She didn't stop until we turned the tape recorder off.

Carolyn Geffel:

I was sitting with her in the kitchen one day in the afternoon—it was a Monday, I know that, because Monday was the day we paid the paperboy. I had her on my lap, and I was feeding her. She was on baby food then—no more bottle—so I can date this for you at around 1960 or very early 1961, probably. Everything was calm, when all of a sudden Adry started to wail. I mean *wail*. She spit up all her mushy strained carrots all over me. I had on a black house dress that I wore rather often. It was a pale blue print when I bought it, and then when it started to fade, I dyed it to get more wear out of it. Black dye covers the best. I was a frugal homemaker—my parents taught me that, by their bad example. They could never handle their money. That's why I ended up so good with numbers. I do all the bookkeeping for our propane business, as you know, and I built up a somewhat impressive wardrobe of black clothes that I dyed at one time or another. On occasion, when I was in town, I'd be mistaken for Amish, if I wasn't smoking.

Adry was *wailing*, and I had orange spew all over my black dress—I looked like a Halloween decoration. She was crying so hard that I didn't realize somebody had been knocking on the screen door. The paperboy was there, and he needed me to pay him for the deliveries for the week. Ordinarily, he would just toss the paper onto the back porch. But on Mondays, he was looking to be paid. Tommy Fermonti was the paperboy then—good-looking boy, like all the Fermontis, and probably a bit of a handful at school, if he was anything like his brothers. He never gave us any trouble, except for making Adry cry when he came to the door.

The next Monday, the same thing happened: Adry burst out crying, and don't you know it, Tommy Fermonti's at the door. This time, I happen to notice that he was playing his transistor radio. It caught my attention, because "Mama Said" was playing, by the Shirelles, and I liked the Shirelles. That was when I started to put things together, and I realized it wasn't Tommy Fermonti that was making Adry cry. It was his radio. She just couldn't stand the sound of the music. It wasn't just "Mama Said," either—everyone has the right to their own taste in music. Greg never cared much for the Shirelles, and that's his prerogative as a person who doesn't know much about music. With Adry, the problem was music in general—all music, or the sound of it.

Nina Oberheimer
(music teacher, Venango County School District):

My name is Nina Gaylor Oberheimer, and I held responsibility for music education in the public school system in Venango County, Pennsylvania, from 1956 to 1986. I graduated from Clarion State Teacher's College in Clarion, Pennsylvania, in 1955, and began my career in education the following year. As I always say, I heard that Clarion call! In my capacity as the music educator for Venango County, I taught all the various instruments—woodwinds, brass, string instruments, and percussion, as well as piano and voice, and, yes, to be clear, I *do* consider the human voice an instrument. I did this for students in all grade levels—K through 8 and up through high school—in the nine elementary schools and two high schools in the district. If you lived in the county for any period in that thirty-year time frame and ever took up a musical instrument in school, I was your teacher. And I hope you've been practicing!

I have a policy of not singling out individual students for praise or criticism. It's too easy to hurt people's feelings and too hard to remember all their names. That being said, I cannot deny that Adrianne Geffel stands out as the most memorable student I have ever had the pleasure to teach. I've had some who are no pleasure, I do admit.

I first became acquainted with Adrianne before she entered school. At the recommendation of her family physician, whom, as I recall, was Dr. Kozcak, the late Dr. Kozcak, I was asked to meet Adrianne and make a professional evaluation of her musical ability. I made a visit to the Geffels' home out on the old Route 6. Although I had been to the location on a few earlier occasions, to purchase propane, I had never before been inside the residential area and never before spoke to either of Adrianne's parents about anything other than my home fuel needs. This was also the first time I ever met the young man of the house, Donny, whom I would have for trumpet lessons for several weeks during his high-school years. The day must have been a Saturday, when I was free from my school duties and available for an extra-curricular adventure such as this. Donny, who was home from school, as well, greeted me at the door, in a manner, and scurried off to fetch his parents from their office on the side of the house. They brought me to join Adrianne in the parlor, where she was sitting blissfully next to one of the chairs, humming to herself.

I listened with great interest to the melody Adrianne was producing, and it was charming. It was clear to me immediately this was a child with an exceptional musical memory. She displayed a high degree of ability to retain music she had apparently heard in the house—an ability all people have, to varying degrees, if rarely on the level of this child at her age. This was combined, in her instance, with a facility for vocal tone production. As I have said, I am one who includes the human voice in the category of a musical instrument. Adrianne at four years of age, because she had not started school yet, was carrying a lovely tune with excellent intonation, up to a point.

In preparation to evaluate the child's musical ability, I brought a portable glockenspiel, a melodica, and a small drum. I sat on the chair near where Adrianne was seated on the floor, and played a simple melody on the glockenspiel, to see if Adrianne would or could hum or play it back. I chose for this the first four bars of Mozart's third variation on "Ah, vous dirai-je, Maman." [Oberheimer hums this music.] By the second note, Adrianne was crying. I continued to play, and she cried more loudly. When I stopped, she reached up and grabbed the glockenspiel off my lap and knocked it onto the floor. It hit the ground so hard that one of the keys broke off. I had to have it replaced, and I paid for the repair myself, so as not to involve the school district, since this was an extracurricular activity.

As I was examining the glockenspiel, assessing the damage, Adrianne started humming again, but it was not a pretty song. The tones were erratic, on-key and off-key in a confusing jumble of notes and noises. There was no discernible pattern and no melody. The rhythms, I could only describe as arrhythmic. Arrhythmic rhythms, atonal tones—if "a-music" were a word, I would use it to describe the sound I was hearing from Adrianne. Let me be clear. It was not "a music," as in *a kind* of music. It was "a-music," as in anti-music. I could barely tolerate the sound of it.

My assessment of Adrianne's musical ability on that day was not as positive as I had initially expected it to be. I could identify a certain talent in the child on the basis of the musicality of the vocal tones she produced in our first moments together. However, her failure to respond to the simple melody I played for her suggested an aversion to music difficult to reconcile with her ability to create musical sounds. I left the Geffels' house that day uncertain of what I had experienced, and yet inclined to suspect I had not encountered the Mozart of Venango County.

When Adrianne entered school, I saw her on an ongoing basis—once every two weeks for the regular classroom music lessons, from kindergarten up to the next grade each year. For the first several years, my time in her company amounted to less than a minute in each session. She was unable to take part in music class with the other students. The sound of other children singing would so disturb her that she needed to be out of the room. Knowing this, her classroom teacher would escort her to the school library, the one place guaranteed to be quiet, while we conducted music class. Eventually, as I assume you have read, I began to work directly with Adrianne, instructing her in piano. That proved to be a fruitful experience for us both and Adrianne, in particular. The time leading up to that was one of confusion and frustration for everyone in Adrianne's life, and also for Adrianne, I can only assume. Her teachers had their hands full—even those who weren't teaching her music.

Annabella Korp (elementary school teacher):

I have only good things to say about Adry Geffel. She was wonderful! All my students were wonderful. You'll never hear anything to the contrary from me. I believe that adults need to believe in young people. Only then will young people believe in themselves. Thank you very much for asking me. I treasure the opportunity to celebrate all my students and demonstrate to them how they can celebrate themselves.

[Korp is asked to assess how Adrianne Geffel's relationship with music affected her performance in the classroom.]

None! None whatsoever. It was not an issue.

Deirdre McAdoo (librarian):

I was school librarian in the First Street Elementary School for four years—four school years, from fall 1966 to spring 1972, so I saw a lot of Adry Geffel. I read your notice in the paper and take it you've talked to her teachers. The only one I know for a fact to still be alive and living in the area is Anna-Bee Korp. She had Adry Geffel for third grade, and then again for fifth grade, after Anna-Bee left the school system and came back—another teacher had been brought in for the third grade, Lou Dragotta, but the fifth grade was open. If you've talked to Anna-Bee, you've heard what a handful Adry Geffel was. She had to take a year off after that third-grade year, just to straighten her head out again.

Adry was with me in the library three or four times a day, sometimes more. Whenever there was any kind of music in the classroom or if one of the kids just started to sing the *Flintstones* theme, Adry would be sent to me. I'm quite sure a few teachers sometimes sent her just to keep the peace in the classroom. Nobody ever really knew when she would hum or sing or hear something she didn't like and break down. Anna-Bee could tell you more about that than I can. She could never really deal with Adry.

Marilyn Schanbaker (cousin):

This was in the newspaper. I'm sure you know the gist of it, though the articles that I saw didn't have everything right. I'll give you the whole story.

Carolyn and I are cousins, as everybody knows. Her mother, my aunt Theresa, and my mother—Carolyn's aunt Helene—were sisters. My mother is still with us, and still keeping her own home—with no help from anybody, except Carolyn and me, when we can get there. Carolyn's own mother passed some years ago, at one point in the midst of everything with Adry, though that had nothing to do with her passing. It may have contributed to her stress, and that's never helpful when you have heart trouble. But I can't see the point in blaming Adry for that.

I came first, a little less than two years before Carolyn, so I'm the older one. People tell me I don't look it—God bless 'em—but I think Carolyn has held up very nicely, for all she's had to deal with. We were named to be like coordinated cousins, Marilyn and Carolyn. When we were teenagers, we even tried to match up the names of our boyfriends, but she got married, even though she's the younger one, and I couldn't find anybody I liked with a name that rhymed with Greg. There was a fun guy in Wilford who I met, and his nickname was Smeg, but I didn't see a big future in that one.

It was 1968. Adrianne was nine years old and home from school for summer vacation. Carolyn and Greg had their heart set on attending the big fuel convention, which was coming to

Harrisburg, and they asked me to watch Adry overnight, so they could go away and they could have a kind of second honeymoon together. I was happy to do it. I was single, as I am to this day, but I never had a problem with kids. The plan was set for Donny to have a sleepover with one of his friends, whoever that was, and I would take Adry for the night.

Well . . . the first day went swimmingly. We spent a lovely day together in my house. We tidied up the kitchen and dusted the furniture together. I showed her how to freshen up the cushions on the sofa by pounding on them like dough. We had a fine old time! I knew how she liked to hum little songs, from Carolyn and everybody else. From time to time during the day, she would hum a little something. It didn't bother me.

I wanted to make something special for dinner, so I made us Rice A Roni, Spanish-style. We were dining pleasantly, together at the kitchen table, and Adry began to hum just about the prettiest song I ever heard. I told her, "That's beautiful, dear." And she said, "I think so, too!"

I said, "What *is* that song, Adry?"

She said, "I don't know—I never heard it before."

I said, "Oh! Really? You never sang it before?"

And she said, "I never *heard* it before now."

I said, "What exactly do you mean, dear?"

She said, "I don't mean anything. I'm just listening to the song, and humming along."

We stopped talking for a minute and just sat and ate, and enjoyed our dinner. I was thinking about what she was saying, and I said, "Adry, sweetheart, are you hearing that music right now?"

She said, "Yes." She looked down and poked at the colored pepper pieces in her rice, and she said, "But it's starting to change now."

That got me thinking, but I never let on to Adrianne that anything was on my mind. We cleared the table and did the dishes. We wiped down the table and mopped the floor, and by then, we were tired from all the day's activities, and I tucked her in. I stayed up a little longer, and made a phone call to my friend Bonnie after Adry was asleep. I knew her husband had a brother in the car business, and I knew he had an older aunt who was a spiritual advisor. I told her, "Bonnie, I need to get the lowdown from you. Is that aunt of your brother-in-law's the real deal? I have a situation here that's out of the ordinary, and I need to get an expert opinion on this. I don't want to be wasting my time with some phony gypsy fortune-teller. I need the real thing."

I said, "Bonnie, you know my cousin Carolyn? I'm watching her daughter, and this is going to sound pretty creepy, because that's exactly what it is, but the girl is *possessed*."

Baucisz Mihaly:

I didn't know Adrianne Geffel at all. Never met her. Never bought a one of her records. My only direct connection to her is not really very direct—the one time Marilyn Schanbaker called me in the middle of the night to ask me about my brother-in-law's aunt

Camille. Marilyn wanted to know if she was a legitimate spiritual advisor. That's how Camille advertised herself. I told her I didn't know what to say, because we didn't really know her very well. We kept our distance from Aunt Camille. She was Chipper's aunt by marriage to an uncle we hardly knew, and the uncle was dead, anyway.

[Note: By "Chipper," Mihaly refers to her husband, Stefan Mihaly.]

I told Marilyn, "I'm not sure what to say to you. She's a spiritual advisor, whatever that is. What—she advises spirits? To me, it's beyond comprehension." That was all Marilyn needed to hear. That was endorsement enough for her. She brought Adrianne Geffel out to see her. The rest was in the newspapers.

Marilyn Schanbaker:

On the morning of the second day I had with Adrianne, I did what I had to do. I made us a nice breakfast of Grape-Nuts fancied up with sliced banana, and I drove Adry out to the county line. It was kind of desolate in those days. Now, it's all built up. There's an Applebee's and a self-storage place and some other modern businesses out there today. But in 1968, there was hardly anything there. We pulled in from the road and drove around to the back, where the parking was.

We walked around the building to the front door, and Madame Camille opened the door for us before we even knocked. "I was *expecting* you . . ."—very dramatic, low, solemn voice. I thought, *Oh boy, here we go. Showtime!* We looked at each other, and Madame Camille burst into a grin, and she said, "I always say that! I just heard your car pulling in. Sit down, please, both of you—sit down."

She put us right at ease. Offered us tea. I don't remember much about the environment. I couldn't see very well. The atmosphere was what you'd have to call moody. The main light, and I think it might have been the only light, came from a couple of candlesticks, which, I noticed, had tiny oval light bulbs instead of wicks. That impressed me. I appreciated that here was somebody who was keeping up with the times.

She was very methodical and helpful. She carefully explained her rates to us and how much each hour would cost and whether we would be paying by cash or check. By now, Adrianne was beginning to get antsy, and she started to make some sounds. I couldn't repeat for you what it sounded like, but it was nervous-like. [Schanbaker hums.] In my house growing up, when there was a thunderstorm, my mother always turned the radio on in the kitchen and kept it playing softly in the background. The signal would crackle and drop off and burst back on. That's the closest thing I can think of to tell you how Adrianne sounded to me.

Madame Camille concentrated all her attention on Adrianne. They sat facing each other at a small round table. Crocheted tablecloth in that pineapple pattern—red. I was there with them, but it was like I wasn't there. Camille reached across to Adrianne and held her two hands. She said, "Let's close our eyes and be totally still and have a moment of silence." Adrianne followed her instructions and sat there without making a sound.

Camille said, "Very good, child." This is all going by my memory, mind you. But this is exactly the same way I told it to the police, so it's official.

Everything was quiet, and Camille said, "Now, let's meditate on the silence. When I say 'meditate,' I mean . . ."—and Adrianne interrupted her.

"I don't hear any silence," she said.

Camille said, "I understand, child—no one can hear silence. Silence is that which we experience when we hear nothing. It cannot be heard. Now . . ."

"I'm not a baby, Miss Camille," Adrianne said, pulling her hands out of Camille's grip. "I'm nine years old. I understand what you're telling me. I'm just telling you that I don't hear any silence." Camille started to say something, and Adrianne interrupted her again. "Not now," she said. "Not now. Not ever."

Camille said, "Oh, well . . . Tell me all about that."

And Adrianne proceeded to tell her everything we all know about her now. She had tried explaining it to her parents and her teachers, she said, but they didn't want to know about it. They were afraid or they didn't believe what they were hearing. The thing is, she heard music in her brain, she said—all the time, she said, or almost all the time—and it changed with her moods. She was feeling pretty nervous at that very moment, she said, and the music was nervous-sounding. She kept talking. She said she didn't mind the music most of the time. She enjoyed being alone, listening to the music playing in her head. But sometimes it was hard to take, like when somebody was playing music at the same time or she got upset and the music became upsetting. She looked at Madame Camille. She said, *Can you help me*?

Camille leaned back in her chair. Adrianne leaned forward. She asked again, this time singing the words in a nursery-rhymey tune, *Can you help me?*

Camille froze. Adrianne asked her again, singing now in a tune that was slightly different—*Can you help me?*

Camille just sat there. Adry asked her one more time, this time singing loud and weird, *Can . . . you . . . help . . . me*?

Camille turned to me and asked me if I would mind leaving the two of them alone. I wasn't sure that was a great idea, but I didn't think it was the worst idea in the world, so I grabbed my purse and got up to go outside. Camille followed me to the front door, and she whispered to me, "Don't you worry. I can cure this girl."

From the outside, I couldn't hear much of what was going on inside. There was talking and talking and more talking. Every now and then, one of their voices got a little louder, and I could make out a few words. Adry was doing some of the talking but was mainly kind of singing—oohing and aahing a strange sort of tune. This got louder and louder. I heard Camille muttering things, and then I heard her clearly say something about "a spirit" or "the spirit." I thought maybe I should go back in, or maybe that would ruin everything. So I stayed outside and paced back and forth.

Adrianne was singing pretty loudly by now, and then I heard some music playing. Camille put a record on. I hadn't seen a record player in there, but evidently there was one, maybe on a shelf I hadn't noticed or a portable. It was classical. Adrianne was still singing. The record was playing, and Adrianne got louder, and her singing got weirder. Camille turned the volume of the record up—*ba bum! Ba bum, ba da bum!!* [Schanbaker simulates the sound.] Adry got louder. Then I heard Camille's voice—"Release this spirit, child! Release this spirit!" Everything got more intense and louder. Camille started to scream, "Release this spirit! Free yourself! Lift this spirit from your soul!"

I turned the doorknob to go in, but the door was locked from the inside. So I ran around to the back, and went in the rear entrance. By the time I entered the room, Adrianne was gone. Camille was standing at the doorway watching as Adrianne was running away, calling for her to come back. "She went wild!" Camille said. "She jumped up and unlatched the door and ran off."

I ran out to catch her, but she was too far ahead of me, and she was awfully fast. Let's face it—she was nine years old, and I was over thirty. I didn't have a chance of catching up with a nine-year-old girl.

I lost sight of her and couldn't tell if she crossed the road and was hiding behind a dumpster or ran into the brush or what. I headed back toward Madame Camille's building and told her, "I'm calling the State Police."

Camille said, "There's no telephone in my salon. Electrical signals disrupt the psychic wavelength."

I said to her, " *'Salon'?!* Is that what you call it? Why don't you just call it a Den of Scary Nastiness to Little Girls and be done with it?" I gave her a piece of my mind. I got in my car and hightailed it out of there to get to a phone booth, and I called the police.

Francis DeAngelese (Pennsylvania State Police officer)

I remember the Geffel case well. I was a young trooper, I was on patrol, and I got a call regarding a possible missing person. I arrived at the location where she was last seen, and I spoke to the proprietor, an individual in the business of psychology or spirituality, that field. She was very concerned about the whereabouts of the Geffel girl and provided a good description of her to me. Another lady met us there shortly thereafter. She was a family member, whose care under which the Geffel girl had been under. She was in an agitated state. I did my best to calm her down but was not very successful. The proprietor of the business stepped in to help, but that only made the family member more agitated. In consideration of the nature of the situation, with a young person possibly missing, I told the ladies I would send out an APB, All Points Bulletin, immediately. The lady who operated the spiritual business offered me the use of her office telephone, and I put out the call.

I inquired about the girl's parents and learned from the family member that they were out of town on business. The dispatcher on duty sent out a message to their location, and they arrived at headquarters within a few hours. They were in a state of acute distress typical of parents of a child potentially missing from a psychology or spirituality business in proximity to the county line. I inquired if anything like this had ever happened before, specifically with the girl. I asked if there were medical issues or medications that the girl might need while she was missing. The parents were cooperative but confused. The mother appeared hesitant to answer on the matter of medical issues. However, the father assured me that the girl was normal and healthy.

We called for support from the local police and canvassed the area where the girl was last seen. When she failed to be located by nightfall, we assigned two officers to patrol the area overnight.

Early the following morning, we received a call from an employee of a paving company in the vicinity. A driver was driving to a job in Happsburg and heard music coming from the back of his truck. He mistook the sound for a faulty radio and drove all the way to Happsburg until he turned off the vehicle and determined that the Geffel girl was in the back of his truck, singing to herself. The girl had found the truck door open, entered the vehicle, and fell asleep on some bags of gravel. I drove out there at high speed and brought the girl to headquarters.

As a result of this incident, county social workers were brought in to look into the home situation with the family, and some years later, after the Geffel girl had grown up and moved out of the area, she sent me a record that she made. She wrote a personal inscription to me on the front, under her picture. I haven't had a chance to listen to the music, but I would presume it has to be enjoyable.

CHAPTER 2

Junior Jam

(1969–1976)

Laurie Emmerich Liebman (social worker):

I was the county agent for youth services in Venango County at the time in question, yes. The majority of the cases I handled were referred to my office by the county and municipal courts, individual administrators in the schools in the district, or law enforcement, as in the case you're asking about. Our office was still fairly new at that time. It was instituted just a couple of years earlier, through an initiative of the federal government under President Johnson that made its way to Pennsylvania. You should study up on this, if you don't know about it already. It was part of the Great Society. We didn't use the term in our office, but Johnson did.

I was right out of school—I went to Haverford College, and everybody *hated* Lyndon Johnson there, because of Vietnam. I had two cousins in the service, and our family was never ultraliberal, so I didn't have a big grudge against Johnson for the war or anything else. If you look into it, you'll see that the Johnson Administration was behind a number of social programs like ours that were created for the benefit of under-privileged and troubled youth—like Adrianne Geffel, not that she was under-privileged. *Troubled*, yes. *Under-privileged*, not exactly—especially if you think of musical talent as a privilege. If you do, you could only call her *over*-privileged.

When I was referred to Adrianne, I knew a good amount of psychology, from college. I had a dual major in business administration and psychology at Haverford. I would pick up more information and tricks of the trade a few years later, when I went for my certification in counselling, which I received in 1974.

The State Police contacted our office after Adrianne had gone missing, was found, and returned to her home. The parents were advised to bring Adrianne to see me for a consultation, and the mother brought her in a few days later. We walked down to the cafeteria in the lower level of the building and spent a couple of hours there. It was an excellent place to hold a meeting, because you could get a soda and a donut or Jell-O if you wanted a treat, and other people couldn't overhear your conversation, because of the buzz from the fluorescent lighting. The three of us sat down, Mrs. Geffel offered me a cigarette, which I accepted, not to be rude on our first meeting, and we talked for about an hour. We both smoked Kents. Adrianne was very respectful and hummed quietly to herself while she wasn't talking. I was prepared for this, having read the police report, and I found the sound so interesting that I wished the lighting weren't quite so loud that day, so I could hear her better.

We had an extremely productive meeting. I learned a great deal about Adrianne and her mother. Mrs. Geffel explained to me how Adrianne heard music in her mind, and she hummed along to what she heard sometimes. Mrs. Geffel told me how she allowed Adrianne to sit by herself, listening to the music she imagined, singing along, while she went about her work. Her mother did the bookkeeping for the family business, she said. I found all this interesting and, it goes without saying, awfully hard to believe.

After an hour together, all three of us, I asked Mrs. Geffel to move down to another table, so Adrianne and I could talk one-on-one. She was utterly cooperative and answered all my questions, sometimes singing her answers in funny little tunes. Making sure not to rush things or cut the session off prematurely, I filled her in on some facts about my own childhood and my musical interests when I ran out of questions for her. In a little while, I called Mrs. Geffel back to join us, I thanked them sincerely for their time, and told them I would phone them in a few days and provide them with my recommendations.

The following day, I went to the library and spent a good hour or two researching psychological disorders. I found several things that related to Adrianne and her mother in certain ways. To be thorough, I sought to corroborate the research material I had gathered with clinical testimony, so I put in a call to my brother's girlfriend, who was a nurse, and got some firsthand input from her. Through this work, I was able to reach a few conclusions about Adrianne Geffel's case. First of all, I had come to feel strongly that Adrianne was *not* possessed by spirits, evil or otherwise, as the woman in the police report had claimed. There was hardly any question in my mind about that.

I telephoned Mrs. Geffel the next day to share my insights with her. Mrs. Geffel asked if she and Adrianne should come to see me again, and I said, as diplomatically as I could, that the two of them were always free to visit me—they didn't need an engraved invitation—but, in all candor, I thought they would be much better off spending time with each other. Adrianne's very problem, I explained, appeared to be a projection of her loneliness. She no doubt felt abandoned by her mother, who was clearly spending too much time on the father's fuel business and not enough time with her children.

I encouraged Mrs. Geffel to organize activities and family outings with Adrianne and her brother. The father could be included, as well, if he was free. Go to the library together. Go to the playground. Go to both places! There was a playground behind the library in those days, before the Seventies and the pedophile scare. Go to church, if you're a churchgoing family. I should clarify, a person's religious affiliation is never my concern as an employee of a government agency. I'm just pointing out, impartially speaking, that unless they weren't religious and Geffel is a Jewish name, church was an option to consider as a family activity.

Carolyn Geffel:

Have you talked to my cousin Marilyn? You probably should. We never really talked again after . . . *Madame Camille.* I see her now and then—we run into each other at the Dollar and Up store, that can't be helped, but we don't talk more than we have to. What is there to say? *Why, thank you so much for bringing my daughter to an exorcist and frightening her so horribly that she slept in a truck! I'm so grateful to you!* My mother, before we lost her, tried to tell me I should be glad for the way things worked out because of that. She had a point, you don't have to tell me. But it pains me to give Marilyn any credit she might possibly deserve.

So you know, we were never a religious household. Greg and I had both our children baptized, at St. John's Lutheran, where I went as a girl, because that was the thing to do—and *why take a chance*? If there really is a heaven and a hell, and your child dies, heaven forbid—I can't believe I just said "heaven," so look, right there—your child dies, of cancer, let's say—face it, no parent would want the kid going through eternal damnation just because they didn't believe in baptism. So, both Donny and Adry were baptized. Adry's godparents, if you want this for the record, were Greg's old friend Jipper Thallen and—and this is funny, her godmother happened to be my cousin Marilyn. Think about that for a moment. She's Adry's godmother, and she doesn't even call me on Adry's birthday.

We hadn't been back to St. John's ever, except for weddings and funerals. But we wanted to give the state person the benefit of the doubt, as an expert in these matters, so we looked up the church schedule in the paper, and we brought Adry to a family social on a Saturday. I thought: *It's on a Saturday, it can't be too-too religious.* The big day for religious activities in the Christian religion is Sunday, which never really made much sense to me. If the Bible says God made Sunday the day of rest, then why would that be the busiest day of the week for God? It shows you that religious teachings don't hold up very well, if you take them seriously.

We arrived at the church at three o'clock in the afternoon, as the paper said, but there was no social. We didn't realize it, but the events of this type were held in the basement of the church, and you had to go through the back entrance to get there. All the regulars were indoctrinated in this, but we were the newbies. Greg and I started walking around inside the church, in hopes of finding someone to help us. He headed toward the front, walking up the aisle on the left, and I poked around the back. There were several little rooms around there. I knocked on the doors—no luck. I opened one or two of them and looked in, if they weren't locked—nobody home. I let Adry stay in the vestibule there, humming to herself.

After a few minutes, I heard someone tinkling around on a piano. I thought, *Oh, good—there's someone here. I'll go back and get Adry, and maybe the person playing piano can help us.* I went back to the vestibule, but no sign of Adry. I looked all around—no Adry. I called out to Greg, and he turned around and came back to me. The two of us looked around together, and I noticed a stairway to the side of the pews, and I headed up the steps. Greg was right behind me. When we got to the top, we found a balcony area with about a dozen folding chairs. There was a piano along the back wall, and Adry was sitting at it, plunking away on the keys. I went to get her, but Greg grabbed the back of my blouse. I stopped and just stood there with Greg.

She didn't know how to play the piano. We never gave her lessons. We didn't even have a piano in the house. We had a record player, and Greg had a radio, but we didn't use them anymore, because of Adry. You know what she was like when music was playing. But this was very different. I don't want to exaggerate to you, even if that's my prerogative as a mother. Adry was not exactly Ferrante and Teicher. She didn't really know what she was doing. But it was *something*, and she was loving it. Greg and I took seats in a couple of the folding chairs and just watched her.

Gregory Geffel:

Through my associations with the many businesses in the county, I was successful in acquiring a high-quality piano for Adrianne's use in our home. Among the clients I serviced was an excavation concern, Saultz Brothers Scrap and Salvage. I alerted Gary Saultz of our interest in a piano for Adrianne, and in less than two months, he told me about an instrument in an old home in town that his company had been hired to clear out for sale. The homeowner, now deceased, was an elderly gentleman—retired English teacher, no family, no heirs, no will. He never married, and—guess what?—he played the piano. Logical. I arranged to purchase the instrument, through Gary, and a crew from Saultz Brothers delivered to us. They had a hell of a time getting it through the front door and into Adrianne's room, I have to tell you. I had to remove the screen door from the front entrance, and that's not as easy as just popping the pin out of the hinge on a regular door. Then, to get the damn thing into her room, I had to pull a strip of case molding off the door frame.

We moved Carolyn's dresser to the side, and the piano fit just right along the wall across from Adrianne's bed. I'm sure you'd like to see it, so I can take you in there later. It's a beauty.

Carolyn Geffel:

The room is technically a guest room now, but we've always called it Adry's room, and the piano is still there. It hasn't been dusted in a week—forgive me for that—but you can see the piano and even play it, if you'd like. I don't suppose you can play any of Adry's music, can you?

[Geffel is answered in the negative.]

I'm not surprised. No offense to you. I don't think many other people can play Adry's music.

Gregory Geffel:

We arranged for Nina Oberheimer to give Adrianne piano lessons on a weekly basis, here in our house. Nina already knew Adrianne, from their earlier encounters here and in school, as you've heard about. Nina advised us to have the piano tuned, and we learned from the tuner that the piano was an outstanding model. I know you'll appreciate this as someone interested in history. It was an Albrecht and Company. I did some research on my own, and that was a very fine German manufacturer based in Philadelphia—top of the line for a piano in its price range.

Nina Oberheimer:

Bryce Mengener, the piano tuner for our area, called me to tell me the Geffels had purchased a piano, and I was stricken with dread. I had a vivid recollection of Adrianne's severe adverse reaction to hearing four bars of Mozart's third variation on "Ah, vous dirai-je, Maman," when I played them for her several years earlier. Over the time after that, I observed her twice monthly as she was escorted from the music classes I led at First Street Elementary School, to reduce the risk of her responding problematically to the music in the classroom. I would not have expected her to take kindly to the sound of a piano. I was uncertain how to reply when Carolyn Geffel came to school on music day to see me and ask if I would provide Adrianne with piano instruction. I consented to try.

I arrived at the Geffel residence late in the morning on a Saturday—my day for enterprise, as I've explained. I walked up to the front door, and I could already hear the piano from a window on the side of the house. It was the sound of a piano, certainly—however, decidedly *not* the sound of music. Mrs. Geffel brought me into Adrianne's room, and I found Adrianne tapping at the keyboard, using only her index fingers. She stopped when she saw us enter, she rose to greet me—her manners were everything her pianism was not—and said, "Good morning, Miss Oberheimer. Would you like to see my piano?" I was very pleased to see her taking pride in her instrument, and relieved that she had stopped playing it. Her mother left us for a moment to fetch a kitchen chair for me to sit in during the lesson. I opted to use the piano bench and offered the chair to Adrianne so she could observe me as I demonstrated the C major scale.

This did not go well. Adrianne started squirming in her chair and making little sounds. I decided in my mind to halt the lesson then and there, and tell Mrs. Geffel, "Okay—I tried." I stopped playing. Then, Adrianne settled down. I looked over at Adrianne, sitting calmly now, and something clicked in my mind.

I got up from the bench and gestured for Adrianne to come back to the piano. I stood behind her, leaning over her, and I lay my two hands on top of hers. I said, "Adrianne, pretend you're a bird, and make two claws with your hands." She did, and I made claws with my hands on top of hers. I held her right hand so her right index finger was over middle C, and I pressed her finger down onto the keys. The sound of the C note rang out, and Adrianne smiled.

We continued working that way, with only Adrianne touching the keys, and the lesson went beautifully—no squirming, no humming, no drama, no trauma for either of us. As long as Adrianne was producing the music herself, the sound posed no apparent difficulty for her. To the contrary, it appeared to give her pleasure.

I continued to provide Adrianne with piano lessons on a weekly basis for eight years, until she left the county for college. I taught her straight through her high school years. The only other piano teacher she ever had during that whole time was the substitute I called in when I could not be available for a lesson—Elizabeth Beener. Mrs. Beener had been *my* piano teacher when I was a young student. She was retired from teaching by this time. She suffered from the gout and lost a fair amount of her hearing. Yet she was able to fill in for me with students who were willing to go to her house for the lesson, past Randall Ridge, and who could play loudly. Mrs. Geffel drove her out there once or twice, and I think Adrianne's older brother Don brought her once, around the time he was driving age. In one way, Mrs. Beener was even better for Adrianne than I, because of her hearing loss. When Adry went off on one of her . . . improvisations . . . it could be hard on the ears.

With Adrianne, I concentrated on technique and music theory in the beginning, and then worked our way up through the piano literature. She developed quickly, because she enjoyed playing. Typically, the student has jumped up off the piano bench before the last note hits the ear, and they're out of the room and out of the house ahead of me. In Adrianne's case, with no exception I can recall, I would hear her playing when I walked up to the front door, and she'd still be playing when I walked back to my car. I should add that she wasn't necessarily playing her lessons when I wasn't in the room with her. She was always much, much, much-much-much more interested in playing her own compositions or improvising, whatever you would call it. Yet, she took well enough to sight-reading and rapidly gained proficiency as a pianist.

One more thing I should add is this, and I don't want to sound unduly critical, because Adrianne was an exceptionally skilled musician, but she generally played with more *feeling* when she was playing her own music, rather than scored music by real composers. She applied herself with discipline to the standard literature, and she could play with great care and precision—I can give you an example. By her third year of study with me, Adrianne was able to play the entire Allemande from Bach's Partita No. 3, perfect to the dotted sixteenth note. Ordinarily, that would be a challenge for a fourth- or fifth-year student, and not everyone would be able to master it. Adrianne did. Nevertheless, her treatment of the piece was distinguished by more precision than emotion. I could see while I was teaching her that she was reserving her emotion for her own music.

Carolyn Geffel:

One good thing about Adry's piano playing, from my point of view as her mother, is, it helped her social life. It gave her an outlet for making music, besides humming, and she seemed happier overall. In her high-school years, it was a definite plus for her to be recognized as a talented girl. It gave her a little status boost. On occasion, another girl or even a boy would come around to hear her play. Her friend Barb even bought her a songbook of pop hits of the Seventies for Adry to play, and Barb would sing along. Barb would come to the house with a shopping bag full of clothes, and she'd dress up like Stevie Nicks or Tina Turner. She'd hold a hairbrush like a microphone, and they'd put on shows together in Adry's room. We could hear them straight through the walls to our business office sometimes. It was like having piped-in music in a doctor's office. They didn't exactly do perfect renditions. Adry had never actually heard the hit records of most of the songs, because she just couldn't take the radio or a record player, so she what she was playing on the piano was the music she read in the songbooks, at least when they started the song. She and Barb would have a ball—they would play and sing and giggle. I could always tell when Adry was really enjoying herself, because she'd take off on one of her musical adventures, forgetting all about the sheet music. You couldn't tell what song she was playing anymore, but Barb would be right there with her, singing the words of the song to the crazy notes Adry started playing or making up her own kooky words on the spot.

Barbara Lucher (friend):

Of course I can tell you about Adry. But why should I? Isn't it interesting that everybody wants to know all about Adry Geffel now? Everybody's looking for her. Everybody wants to know, where'd she go? What's she doing? What's she thinking? Uh-huh. Fine and dandy. Isn't that sweet? So thoughtful.

Would you like to ask me some questions? I bet you would. I'll talk to you—I'm sitting here, aren't I? We didn't come to Panera's for the fucking gluten-free bread. I'll answer your questions, but I have one for you first: Where were all you people when Adry really needed somebody to talk to? Explain that to me.

[Lucher is prompted to offer her own explanation.]

And you're going to answer whatever I ask you with another question? Is that how oral history works?

[Lucher is welcomed to offer her own view on this. Lucher laughs.]

That's pretty fucking funny. [Lucher continues laughing.]

I'll tell you something about Adry: She wouldn't like *this* one bit. She was a sensitive woman—strong *and* sensitive. Do you get that? Doesn't matter. That's how she was.

I bet you don't know much about Adry—I'm talking about the *real* Adry. Who have you talked to? Her brother Donny? He never knew her, not really—he wouldn't let himself. It might get in the way of making fun of her behind her back—I saw him do it. We all ate in the same lunchroom, and I had friends in his grade. Know what he called her, behind her back? "Craz-dry." Stupid. Cruel. Not even a good joke.

Did you talk to his parents? *Big help!* They can give you the facts, for sure. Birthday: May 19. High-school graduation: June 1977—we sat together at the convocation, way in the back, behind everybody else, where they put us, so we weren't in the pictures. Mr. and Mrs. Geffel can give you all the facts. But you tell me this: What did her parents ever give *her*—besides the piano? That was a great thing, no question there. But it took them years to figure out that maybe, if you're raising a musical genius, you could get her an instrument to play. And they never ever understood what she was *doing* when she played.

We were best friends in high school. But I wasn't her *only* friend or the only girl who could have been her friend. Other girls liked her—Adry was likable—but everybody was always nervous with her and afraid she might suddenly burst into song, just because, because that's what Adry did. We met in the library, where I always went during study hall, because I liked to read, which made me something of a weirdo at our school, and Adry was there because that's where they sent her to keep her quiet or quiet as they could keep her. So Adry and I, the two weirdos, made friends in the library. We made funny faces at each other and passed notes. I felt like we were secret agents.

I missed her when she left. I really missed her, a lot.

[Lucher is asked to elaborate.]

What did I miss about her? Is that what you want to know? Is that your idea of a *probing* inquiry? I missed *everything* about her. I missed her laugh. She had a laugh . . . it always reminded me of TV cartoon music. You know, Sylvester lays a nasty trap for Tweety Bird and then steps into it himself—*wee*-wah! That was Adry's laugh—sort of. I can't do it justice. I missed her smile, that was kind of crooked and quavery, like it could burst wide open any second. I missed her *eyes*. You never met her, so you wouldn't know, and none of the photographs, not even the Avedon, capture the look of Adry's eyes. It was really fucking *strong*—like, steeeeely. Not distant or cold, but hard and bright as steel, until something made her laugh or got her upset, and her eyes would swell up and get as big as the world.

I missed talking to her. We talked about everything—books we both read, things we saw on TV. Adry watched the nightly news—she watched the fucking *news*. I never knew another kid who ever watched the fucking news if it wasn't for homework. She was interested in the world, and it was good for her that the news had no background music. "Theme from *Shaft*"—[Lucher simulates sound of electric guitar with wah-wah effect]—and then no music for half an hour, just right for Adry.

We both liked Austen—Jane Austen, not Steve Austin from *The Six Million Dollar Man*, who just wasn't our type. We read through all six of the Austen novels—*Emma* twice, just to see if we could find things we didn't catch the first time. That made us want to read every book we ever read twice. But there just wasn't the time. The library had only one copy of every book, so we couldn't both read the same book at the same time in two different houses. We had to hand the one copy we had back and forth to each other and take turns reading it, or read the same page together in Adry's room. We did that as often as we could do it, lying on Adry's bed.

She saved my ass in English class once, in sophomore year. We had Mrs. Riggio. I sat behind Adry. Riggio was blathering some bullshit about John Steinbeck, and I whispered to Adry, "Fuck her." Riggio heard me and yelled out, "Who said that?" Adry answered, "That was me. I said 'Faulkner'—William Faulkner.

I'm sorry for the outburst, but Faulkner was a superior writer, more of a modernist, and surely more deserving of the Nobel Prize for Literature than Steinbeck. Don't you agree, Mrs. Riggio?"

She was fucking funny, and I don't mean just *weird* funny. When she disappeared, I missed her so much I could barely stand it. I had to get away myself, just to keep myself together. So I did some travelling for a while—for quite a long while, actually. I didn't come back till my mother died, in February, and that's the only reason I even got your letter. I wish I never opened it.

Beth Platt (high-school classmate):

She was weird. I loved that. We were in Health together, sophomore year and junior year, and Chem, junior year. I always tried to get a seat in front of her, so I could hear her humming when the class got hard. It was like having my own human radio. My favorite was learning the Hess cycles and those concepts. That really got Adry going. For years after, I couldn't go to a Hess station without hearing Adry humming in my head.

Donald Geffel:

As a person who's three years older than my sister, I was always more advanced. I was driving age three years before her. I already had a car of my own, a '75 AMC Pacer, orange-gold—only thirty thousand miles on it when I got it, and not a scratch from the first owner's accident after the body work was done. I gave Adry lots of rides when she needed them. I took her all the way to the north side of Randall Ridge for a piano lesson once and waited there in the car for her for forty-five minutes. I'm not complaining. If you have to wait for forty-five minutes in a car, a Pacer is the way to go—with those giant windows, it feels like you're not even in a car. I took her to the shopping center, to Shopping Town, when she wanted to shop. I even chauffeured her to the junior dance with her friend Barb Lucher, and I had to wait in the parking lot for two hours and fifteen minutes for them. There were some kids driving age in the other cars in the lot, screwing in their vehicles, and I didn't need to see that. It's the one time I wished I didn't have a Pacer.

Barbara Lucher:

Junior year, time for the spring dance—the Junior Jam, short for Jamboree. Even the squares in the class know better than to use the word "Jamboree." Everybody's running around, fussing and planning. Adry and I, as official class weirdos, take our rightful place above it all and act like we have no time for such trivial adolescent frivolity. Ronny Fermonti asked me to go with him. I blew him off. Better that than having to actually blow *him*. Dennis Schoenberg asked Adry. He wasn't a bad guy, and not too stupid. Adry might have gone with him if I were going, too, and if it weren't for the tiny matter of the fact that the Junior Jam was a fucking dance, and dances have music. Adry couldn't have taken the sound of all that music.

I went over to her house. We raided the kitchen cabinets for snacks and munched down a feast of Cheetos and Cokes. We just hung out and didn't talk at all about the dance. We were in her room, figuring out what to do next, and I said, "What would you wear if you went?"

Adry opened up her clothes closet—it wasn't very big—and started pulling out things that would be fun to put together in a sort-of-nice, sort-of-silly way. She had a super-hot off-the-shoulder peasant blouse with billowy sleeves that was maybe her favorite thing and for sure my favorite thing to see her in. She held it against her front with one hand and took down a shiny black fake-leather vest with long fringes on the bottom and pressed it on top of the blouse with her other hand, and she struck a goofy glamour pose in the mirror on her dresser. I went behind her, pulled out a pair of earplugs I bought at the drug store that day, and waved them next to her ears. Adry broke into that crooked smile of hers. I yelled through the door to Donny's room, "Can you drive us to the high school?"

In my head, I had calculated that the milling around part of the Jam was probably over by now, so Adry wouldn't have to deal with trying to carry on conversations with people while music was playing in the background. Her head would have exploded. We got to the school around the time the dancing started. I ceremoniously removed the earplugs from their plastic case and wriggled them into Adry's ears. We got to the door to the gym, and she stopped and said, "I can still hear a little of the music through these earplugs." I said, "Fear not—I have further provisions." I patted her hair down over her ears, then took a long scarf out of my purse that I had liberated from my mother's wardrobe for the night. I wrapped it around her head, covering her ears—three full times—as stylishly as I could. I clapped my hands a couple of times next to her right ear. Adry shook her head as if to say, "No—nothing," and we walked in the gym, arm in arm.

The beat of the music throbbed through the room so physically that nobody really needed to hear the music to dance. Adry and I just followed the people around us, and we danced, and we danced, and we danced. We grooved along to whatever they were playing—Earth, Wind and Fire and Elton John—"Shining Star," "Philadelphia Freedom"—David Bowie, "Fame," "Kung Fu Fighting" by whoever that was by. Super-fucking great fucking music! We never got off the dance floor. People danced around us, and lots of people waved or yelled out greetings to us, which nobody could hear over the music, so nobody realized Adry couldn't hear a thing.

The night wound down—slow dance time—and they put on Frankie Valli, "My Eyes Adored You." And Janis Ian, "At Seventeen"—a seriously odd song to play there, but it was a big hit, and the vibe and the tempo were perfect for slow dancing. We stayed on the floor and kept dancing, holding each other close. Adry's head was nestled close to mine. My mouth was just an inch from the scarf wrapped around her ears. I was sure she couldn't hear me, and I whispered, "I love you, Adry Geffel."

CHAPTER 3

Models and Muggers

(1977–1978)

Ruth Sirotta LeMat
(violist, music educator, and widow of
Pierson LeMat, Juilliard instructor):

I met my late husband Pierson in the summer of 1965. We were students. I was attending the Curtis Institute of Music in Philadelphia. I was a viola student and was graduated two years later, in 1967, with a BM—a bachelor of music degree, not the potty term. My late husband was about to enter his final year of study at the Cleveland Institute of Music in Cleveland, Ohio, as a student of piano pedagogy and performance. We met at Tanglewood. Both our schools had organized trips there, as many conservatories do, and, consequently, that's where we met. I wrote a poem about this, which I read at Pierson's memorial concert at the Juilliard Theater on the evening of November 14, 2007. I've always wondered if Adrianne Geffel might have been there that night, in disguise.

Pierson was a member of the piano faculty at Juilliard when Adrianne applied for admission to the school. He was decidedly *instrumental* in her being admitted, if you'll forgive the pun. I had more than a little to do with that. I was teaching theory and composition at the School of the Arts at New York University, where I would teach until my retirement four years ago. As two musicians and music educators, Pierson and I talked often of our trials and tribulations—and our triumphs. I would most certainly consider Adrianne Geffel to qualify in every category.

In that period, the faculty at Juilliard had the primary responsibility for student admissions. There were demonstrable benefits to this system. For instance, a faculty member who had been teaching a pupil in private lessons could more or less have that person admitted without panicking over it. I could pass along a student of mine to Pierson or recommend the child of a friend, and the student would be accepted without going through all kinds of ghastly red tape. It was so much more *convivial* than it became after the legal people got involved.

One night, Pierson came home and told me he had received an application from a very interesting girl in Pennsylvania. Since I had attended conservatory in Philadelphia, Pierson was curious to know if I had ever heard of the young lady's piano teacher, whose name I don't recall anymore—I'm sorry. I had never heard of this instructor, and I've had no reason to retain her name. Customarily, if someone on the Juilliard faculty was friendly with the applicant's private teacher, the applicant was a shoo-in.

Adrianne had submitted a tape recording with the application. She made a cassette tape. This was fairly novel at the time. It subsequently became standard practice in the screening processes for all the conservatories I know, and eventually, students would start sending videos. In those days, the fact that Adrianne had recorded a cassette made her stand out, as did the fact that she had sent in the application fee in cash bills. Pierson brought the tape home, but, to his credit, did not keep the cash for himself. He played the tape on the cassette machine we had for recording lessons in the house. At one point, he called me into the room and replayed a part of it for me to hear. Adrianne had recorded three pieces: a Bach fugue, a Chopin étude, and a third piece neither Pierson nor I could identify. It was decidedly modern, unorthodox but compelling, and Adrianne's performance of the work had great feeling and also displayed excellent technique. Pierson said something on the order of "Sounds like she can play."

I told him, "I'd be curious to know who composed that last piece."

Pierson said, "Is it possible this girl wrote it herself?"

I said, "If she's a composer on that level, you should bring her in—or I will."

Pierson said, "She didn't apply to NYU. You can't have her."

We read the label on the cassette and found the names of the three composers—Bach, Chopin, and Geffel. The third one of them was approved to audition before the Juilliard faculty.

Carolyn Geffel:

I was determined that my daughter Adry would go to college, and not just because I never got to go myself. I've done just fine without a college degree, since we own our own business and I haven't had to fill out a million job applications and check "none" on the line about college and end up missing out on the opportunities I could have had if only I were a college graduate. I dreamed of my daughter fulfilling my dream, if it's okay to dream about a dream, and see her march onto the campus of Cedar Crest College. I helped her fill out her application for CCC and happily wrote out the twenty-five-dollar check for the fee. To be thorough, we picked a safety school, too—Venango County Community College, VCCC. It was Adry's own idea—Adry and her friend Barb Lucher, it was their idea—to apply to Juilliard, though I had nothing against that. She paid the application fee herself, out of money she had saved up from babysitting.

Nina Oberheimer:

I believed that Adrianne had the talent to follow in my footsteps and study music at Clarion State Teacher's College. I could practically hear that Clarion call ringing for Adrianne as it had rung for me. I let Adrianne know all about Clarion and what makes it the special place it is—the peaceful setting off to the side of Route 9, the full half-floor of classrooms for music, art, and drama right below the ground floor of the Humanities and Sciences Building, the lively cafeteria life, and the fine instructors, many of whom had advanced degrees in the subjects they were teaching. I said, "Don't take my word for it, Adrianne—the proof is standing right in front of you. Clarion may not be Juilliard, but . . ."

Adrianne said, "What's Juilliard? If Clarion isn't Juilliard, what *is* Juilliard?"

I told her, "Well, you can look it up in the encyclopedia." And so she did. The next time I saw Adrianne, all she wanted to talk about was Juilliard—Juilliard-*this* and Juilliard-*that*. She told me she had decided to apply—she had made up her mind, and would I be so kind as to write her a letter of recommendation? I thought, *Well, I don't want to be the one to burst the girl's balloon. That's the Admissions Department's job.* I wrote a glowing letter for her, of course—I thought, if she wants so badly to go to Juilliard, I should help her however I can, and it could make all the difference to have a letter of recommendation in my name, with my credentials on it.

Barbara Lucher:

So Adry comes over to my house. She says, "I want to go to Juilliard."

I say, "Alrighty then—let's go to Juilliard!"

She says, "I have to apply first. It's a music school."

So we got crackin'. She'd sent away to the school for information, and brought over this pile of pamphlets and forms to fill out. You were supposed to list all the awards you got and concerts you gave at Carnegie Hall or whatever-the-fuck. Okay—*right*. Adry'd been playing piano in her bedroom for her teacher and me. She'd performed for precisely two people in her life—three if you count her mother, three and a half if you count her fuck-shit brother Donny. Her father didn't count. For anything. So we got the idea to tape her with the cassette recorder I got for Christmas from Radio Shack and send the cassette in to show the pointy-heads at Juilliard what the girl could do.

The paperwork she got listed some music you were expected to be able to play, so Adry practiced up, and I recorded her. We taped two things—classical stuff, unbelievably impressive. She finished, I pushed the OFF button, and I just looked at her. I said, "Can you imagine living in New York? People everywhere! Models! Muggers! Homosexuals! Subways! Broadway! Deejays! Museums! Street gangs!"

Adry got that expression in her face that she got when the music was bubbling up in her—that super-focused look, like here comes the music, get the fuck out of my fucking way! She started playing the piano, and I just watched her and listened. The first time she stopped for a second, I hit the RECORD button on the recorder. I got my face in front of her and looked her straight in the eye and started mouthing words to her, without actually saying anything out loud: *Models! Muggers! Homosexuals!* I kept going with everything I could think of when I thought about

New York: *Skyscrapers! Pickpockets! Fancy clothes! Beggars! Jazz!* And Adry kept playing—kind of following the words I was giving her, kind of in her own world. The music was incredible—abso-fucking-lutely incredible. That's the only way to describe it. You know what I mean when I say "incredible"? Okay. Then, take that, and multiply it *abso-fucking-lutely* times.

Adry sent in the cassette with everything we recorded, including the last thing. She got called in to do an audition in person at the school, and I went with her and drove. We borrowed my aunt Connie's Datsun. Aunt Connie was pretty much out of it and didn't even ask where we were going. Adry's mother made a big show of offering to drive Adry in herself—this *was* her daughter going to interview for college—but it was pretty obvious to me that she was relieved not to have to make that long drive and find her way around New York City. She did pack us bag lunches, that she did, and she gave Adry the hugest hug I ever saw her give her, when we were leaving. Ooooooh—so *sweet*! She held onto Adry for so long it was like she would never see her again. She was only about ten years off.

I packed a pair of earplugs for Adry to use if she found herself around other students playing instruments—we figured there might just be a little bit of music at a music school. And in case the earplugs didn't quite do the job, I brought along my cassette recorder and the headphones I used for listening to records on my stereo. The cassette recorder had a shoulder strap, so you could carry it like a handbag. I told Adry, "Just put on the headphones and plug them into the recorder. I have a blank tape in there. Press

PLAY, and you won't hear a thing but maybe a humming sound. Just pretend you're listening to music." I knew nobody would actually listen to a cassette with headphones and walk around that way, but it was the only scheme I could come up with without stealing a drawerful of my mother's scarves.

We got to Juilliard, eventually. I found a parking garage like fifty fucking miles from the school, and we got to the audition just in time. They wouldn't let me be there for the actual audition and interview she had to do, so I went outside and walked around the area. I suppose since you're such an expert on cultural history, you've been to Lincoln Center. You know—just across the street from Juilliard there's this grand fountain, like a postcard from Rome. There's the opera and the ballet. There's the philharmonic orchestra. I could feel it in the air that I was in the heart of high art in New York City. I didn't give half a shit about any of that, and my time was limited, so I went across the street and had a quick beer in a tavern there. The drinking age in New York was only 18 in 1977. So I was just a couple of months from being legal.

I get back to Juilliard, and Adry is out of her audition and sitting in the waiting area, pretending like she's listening to music with my headphones and cassette recorder. I ask her how it went, and she says, "I think okay. They just told me to wait out here." We sit there together for what feels like twenty fucking years. There's lots of other students and parents sitting around us, staring at each other. Adry gets a little antsy and starts pacing around the room, still with my headphones on and recorder hanging from her shoulder. One of the fathers, an Oriental guy—there were a bunch of families from Japan and China and Korea and the rest—he comes over to me, and he says, "Excuse me—I'm sorry, but I'm curious about your friend. Can you tell me, what is she doing with that electronic equipment?"

I say, "She's just listening to music."

He says, "Music—on a cassette? Listening with headphones? While she's walking?"

I say, "Yep. You have a problem with that?"

He says, "No, no—thank you. I never saw that before." He hands me his business card and walks away.

I'm reading the card and trying to guess what "Sony" is, when a lady with a clipboard comes out and calls Adry's name. Adry pulls off the headphones and walks up to her. I go over to them and stand behind the lady while they talk. The lady says, "You've qualified for a second audition. You can play one more piece for us, and it can be any composition of your choosing."

Adry stands there thinking. Looking over the lady's shoulder, I lock eyes with Adry and start mouthing words to her.

The lady starts writing on her clipboard. She says, "And what is the title of the piece you'll be playing?"

Adry says, "Models and Muggers."

Alton A. Herschon (Juilliard piano faculty, retired):

I served dutifully, if not pleasurably, on the faculty committee that considered Adrianne Geffel for admission to Juilliard. If she entered the school in the fall term of 1977, as you say, her audition would have taken place in the month of March that year. I believe my vote was determinative in this instance. To be candid, I was not persuaded of Miss Geffel's ability in the first of her auditions. If I'm not mistaken, she played Chopin's Étude, Op. 25, No. 3, in F major—an interesting selection, don't you think? As you know, Chopin dedicated the piece to Marie Catherine Sophie, Comtesse d'Agoult, who was Franz Liszt's mistress. Miss Geffel's performance had a certain polish but lacked nuanced sensitivity to the adulterous subtext of this étude. I gave her a passing score, but not a high score, for the first round.

In her second audition, I found Ms. Geffel's playing to be more emotively expressive. Needless to say, I loathed the piece she chose to play. It was discordant and maladroitly constructed. That Ms. Geffel selected such a work, with centuries of superior music at her disposal, was a bafflement to me. Nevertheless, her performance of the piece, in the fullness of its loathfulness, was exemplary. She played with such precision that she made the utter irrationality of the music ringingly clear. Her touch at the keyboard was meticulously controlled, from the gratuitous passages of pianissimo to the arbitrary fortissimo. Most impressively, she played with a depth of feeling that a lesser pianist would be unable to bring to music so resolutely inexplicable.

At the conclusion of the audition, the members of the committee voted on Ms. Geffel's candidacy, one after another. I was the first to vote, as always, being the person seated furthest to left, nearest the exit door. I voted "yea" to admit. By the rules of admission in place at the time, a majority vote was required for acceptance. Accordingly, Ms. Geffel would still have been accepted for admission if I had voted “nay,” but the vote would *not* have been unanimous. Hence, without my vote in her favor, her acceptance would not have been unanimous. I made certain to let her know this several years later, when she achieved acclaim as a musician.

Barbara Lucher:

We left there and had no fucking clue if she was accepted or not. The letter from the school came in the mail later. We went for a walk to shake out the Juilliard dust and see the sights of New York. I don’t know which way we went, honestly, but we crossed one street, and we were in a pretty sketchy part of town. It was like *The Wizard of Oz* in reverse—we walked out of the color world and into the black and white. There was a bar with an Irish name, front painted all green about a hundred years ago, and now it was just shit-brown-former-green. We thought we should celebrate—or drown our tears, one or the other, we didn’t care. So we went in and had a couple of drinks. Whiskey sours, don’t ask me why—the words just sounded so *New Yorky*. After a while, we looked outside, and it was dark. Adry said, “Oh, God—what are we going to do now?” All of it sudden, it dawned on us that we still had a seven-hour drive home, and I was a little woozy.

There was a pay phone in the corner. I broke a couple of bills and got change from the bartender and called my house. My mom answered, as always. My loser-ass father didn't know where the telephone *was*. I said, "Big news! Adry's audition went great! She's talking to the people right now, and she told me to call you so you can call her mother so she doesn't worry. They're going to give her a tour of the school in the morning—isn't that stupendous? They have free rooms at the school for us to stay overnight, so we'll see you all tomorrow. Bye!" And I hung up. Adry just shook her head at me and smiled that crinkly smile of hers and ordered another round of whiskey sours.

The school didn't really have free rooms for us. Anybody would know that but my mother. And we sure as hell didn't have enough money for a hotel. So we kind of waddled our way to the parking garage where I left my aunt Connie's Datsun. I think we walked around ten different blocks till we found the place. We had to go past this ticket-taker guy in a glass booth by the entrance, and he gave us the big once-over as we stumbled by. We made it to the car and crawled in the back together and locked the car doors with a big whack. We were all giggly and feeling fan-fucking-fabulously adult and irresponsible. We curled up on the back seat—our own personal haven in New York City for the night—and the two of us just laid there, snuggled and quiet for a very long time. I was pretty lightheaded and watched the roof of the car slowly spinning around. After a while, I closed my eyes and said, "Good night, Adry," and I felt her kiss my hair. And . . . well, you're a big boy.

I have no clue what time it was, but there was a rap on the side window of the car. I opened my eyes. There was a little daylight in the garage, and the ticket guy from the front was glaring down at us. He waved his wristwatch at us and gave us the pointy-thumb sign to get the fuck out of there. I guess his shift was over, and he must have been keeping an eye on our car all night, to make sure we didn't get robbed or raped or killed or all of the above. He was a skeleton of a guy with like two teeth in his mouth—the scariest thing I saw in New York—but he was alright.

As everybody knows, Adry was accepted at Juilliard, and she went there for a while. I drove her in and helped her carry her stuff and get set up in her student housing place—it was a room in part of an old hotel or haunted house that Juilliard was renting out or some weird New York arrangement like that. I had to turn right around, because I didn't go to college, and I was working nights at the Denny's. But I ended up keeping my aunt Connie's Datsun—I never returned it to her, so she gave it to me, you could say. So I was able to drive in and visit Adry sometimes.

Brenda Magnoli-Schuschert (Dean of Student Life, Juilliard):

I joined the Juilliard administration in the academic year of 1982–83 as an Assistant Dean, and I was promoted five years later, in '87–88, to Associate Dean of Student Affairs. It was a new position, of my own initiation, and from there, in '90–91, I was appointed the first Dean of Student Life at the Juilliard School. Historically, before I came to Juilliard, the policy was to address considerations of student life as the need arose. In the absence of student life as we would recognize it, the need was never deemed to arise.

Speaking historically, once again, the Juilliard experience was a fairly solitary one. Students were expected to dedicate themselves entirely to the music. They were required to practice their instruments, and beyond that, to be breathing. For the administration of the school—and by extension, for the young musicians at the institution they were administering—student life was conceived as the fact that the students were alive, and that was all the school required of them. That and practice. A great deal of practice. Long, long, lonely hours of practice.

Having arrived when I did, I never had the privilege to know Adrianne Geffel in the brief time she was a student here. However, I did get to meet her once, after a concert she gave for the benefit of the New Music Society of America, at the 92nd Street Y. This was 1981. She had become quite the phenomenon by then. There was a reception, and a large crowd was gathered around her. I waited my turn to pay my respects—I introduced myself as a dean at her near–alma mater and told her how much I enjoyed the concert. I made a friendly quip about not *understanding* it but finding it fascinating. There were so many people talking around us that she must not have heard me, because she didn't respond.

F. Dieter Wundt (piano instructor, Juilliard):

Of course I remember Adrianne Geffel. She was an unusual case. I provided her individual piano instruction when she was a first-year student at Juilliard.

My ideas on the pedagogy of piano performance are well

established. I refer you to my many books on the topic. I recommend you begin with the first volume in my series, *Muscle Unbound: Toward a Physiology of the Mechanics of Keyboard Technique, Vols. 1–7.* I would imagine that for your purposes as an interviewer of musicians, a familiarity with the first several volumes would suffice.

As I note in each of my books, piano technique is a mechanical science. My work builds upon and improves greatly upon the ideas of the fledgling theorist of musical science, Otto Ortmann, who taught that the laws of mechanics—action and reaction, equilibrium of forces, dependence of a force upon mass, and the acceleration laws of the lever—apply to physiological motion as well as to mechanical motion in general. The human body is a machine, much like the piano itself. However, as I have pointed out in my work, the piano is not a human body. It need not be caressed, fondled, provided affection. As a machine, the piano is in every way superior to a man—or, for that matter, a woman. For a musician in performance, working in competition with the instrument, intimidation is inevitable.

Musical notation is nothing more than data to be translated into sound by the transfer of mechanical energy from one machine, the human body, to another, the piano. I require of my students to process the data before them in the form of a musical score with the unerring precision and unyielding indifference of a machine. To do this successfully, the musician needs to repress all human emotion and adhere to the purely mechanical task of playing the notes. When Adrianne Geffel read music, she was able to do this sufficiently well for a short duration. I observed her with great satisfaction as she would open the score, shake her head clear, and attempt to shut down emotionally. She had the capacity to play every note correctly, wonderfully devoid of feeling, for a brief period. Unfortunately, she would inevitably lapse and give in to her emotions. She would soon begin to play material not on the page, at which point I would cut the lesson short. This occurred fairly often, as a matter of fact. She withdrew from my class after a small number of sessions.

Andres Appelbaum (Juilliard classmate):

Didn't know her well, to be honest. Wish I did! Nice, pretty, quiet. Adrianne Geffel—the mystery girl. None of us heard her music till the First-Year Recital, so we had no idea who she was, really. She was just this *mystery* girl.

I asked her out once, kind of. I thought it was a date. Not sure she agreed. Outdoor concert in the bandshell at Lincoln Center, across the street from school. The Sylvan Wind Quintet, playing Stamitz and Dahl. I knew it would be fun. We met there, concert started—casual atmosphere, outdoors, warm night. We're chatting between the selections. And . . . she's staring at my lips when I'm talking to her. I'm thinking, *Oh, wow—this girl really likes me.* She's checking out my mouth! *Oh, wow . . .* We're watching the concert, and she pulls her hair back for a second and scratches her ear, and I see that she's wearing earplugs and probably can't hear a note of the music. She's reading my lips, just to figure out what

I'm saying to her. And that was my big date with her—Adrianne Geffel, the mystery girl.

Biran Zervakis (Juilliard classmate):

I want to say something first, before you ask me anything. I need to make something completely clear. My relationship with Adry, however you'd define it—and who can truly define a relationship between two people, or any number of people?—it was . . . [Zervakis pauses to drink from a bottle of water.] I can't put it in words. Words cannot describe it. It was something that happens just once in a lifetime, for those who are lucky enough to live the lifetime I've had. Adry and I were . . . *us*. Whatever that was, whatever words you would choose to use to describe that *thing*, those words would be inadequate. I just want to make that clear.

This is for a real book, right? Not just a school project? Nothing against school—I had the great gift of meeting the magnificent Adry in a school, when we were both young students at Juilliard. I just want to know if this is for a master's thesis or a dissertation that two old professors will glance over to keep their tenure before the thing is filed away in the basement of a library—I just want to know, because my time is valuable.

[Zervakis is assured that the interview is being conducted for a book for prospective publication.]

Alright—just a note, since this is going to be printed: My first name—it's pronounced "Byron," like Lord Byron, but it's spelled . . . and be sure to get this right—write it down . . . [Zervakis stops talking until the interviewer has a pencil in hand to write.] B-I-R-A-N—Biran. *Not Brian*, for God's sake—Brian's just my legal name. [Zervakis takes a deep breath and has another drink of water.]

Adry and I . . . *Adry and I* . . . I have to say that again—I so love the sound of it. *Adry and I* . . . first met in the hallowed halls of the Juilliard School. Adry was studying piano, by the way, and I had recently begun to study the cello, with the kind encouragement of my maternal grandmother, who knew about the instrument from being on the Board of Directors at Lincoln Center. I would watch Adry reading in the lounge or walking between classes. I loved the way her headphones bobbed back and forth when she moved. Whenever I would see her heading toward the piano practice rooms, I would follow her there, and while she was playing, I would watch from behind her back through the little window on the door. I could feel the connection between us for months before we ever spoke.

The two of us would talk at school sometimes, of course, though we didn't need to say much or have the occasion to. After a while, when we passed each other, I would say "Hi," and she would answer in exactly the same way. There was something there that was so special that it would have been virtually undetectable to anyone, even to Adry herself.

Ruth Sirotta LeMat:

Pierson [LeMat's late husband] took Adrianne Geffel on as a piano student in the second or third month of the fall term. She had been with Dieter Wundt, and that was a failed endeavor. Dieter's approach to piano technique was terribly limited. Practically all he cared about was muscles, whereas Pierson was concerned not only with the muscular system, but with skeletal structure, as well. He was thought of as broad-minded.

Pierson gave his lessons in our apartment. As a result, I had the opportunity to meet Adrianne Geffel and observe her at the piano. I got to know her very well over time. If I was home during the lesson, I always offered Pierson's students a cold drink and something sweet. Adrianne and I sat together in the dinette, and we talked. I liked her very much. She always had a book with her, whatever she just happened to be reading. She had an active inner life—some would say overly active, especially when she was making music. I didn't see her that way.

In the spring term, Pierson was guiding Adrianne in preparation for the First-Year Recital, in May. If memory serves, Adrianne was working up Beethoven's "Fifteen Variations and Fugue in E-flat major, Op. 35." Adrianne liked to play a couple of pages of the piece, then take a break and improvise. This was highly unorthodox. It frustrated Pierson to no end. One day I told him, "Pierson, darling—what's the harm? Let the girl blow off her steam. Besides, her improvisations are remarkable—and don't forget, Beethoven also like to improvise." He consented to permit her to work this way. In time, I believe, he grew to look forward to hearing the improvisations. I surely did.

As she progressed in her preparation for the recital, I knew she was getting anxious. The last day she was in our house, I gave her a drink and a piece of pound cake. She poked at the cake with her fork, and she said, "Mrs. LeMat, can I tell you something?"

I said, "Of course, Adrianne. What is it?"

She said, "When I play the fifteen variations, I hear another hundred in my head."

I said, "Play them, Adrianne—*play them*." And she took a huge bite of pound cake and devoured it.

Barbara Lucher:

Next question. I don't want to talk about that [Geffel's First-Year Recital]. I wasn't there. I couldn't make it. I *wanted* to go. I *planned* to go and told Adry I would be there. Then, the very fucking same fucking day, my loser-ass father takes it upon himself to give his sister Connie *my* car. Yeah, yeah—it used to be her car, but now it was my car. She never asked for it back, as far as I know. If she asked him for it, I didn't know anything about that. How could I be expected to know that? I didn't wiretap his fucking phone.

And now, at the last minute, I have no way to get to New York for Adry's recital. I left a message for her at the school. That's all I could do, and I really don't want to talk about this. It was the first time I ever let Adry down.

Biran Zervakis:

The recital is etched forever in my memory. You can put that down in those exact words—I like that. I chose to play an excerpt from the Brahms Sonata for Cello and Piano in F major, Op. 99, because I knew it would be excellent for Adry and I to do as a duet. She would have done it with me and it would have been beautiful in every way, for sure, if I had asked her. It was a shame I was obliged to play it with one of my teachers, Paul Andrade, at the piano, because he insisted on trying to help me.

Everyone in the recital was told to meet backstage [in the Juilliard Theater] beforehand. Adry hadn't arrived yet, and one of the teachers called out, "Adrianne Geffel? I have a telephone message for Adrianne Geffel." Wanting to be helpful, I said, "I can take that. I'm her friend. I'll give it to her."

Adry showed up right before the start time and took a seat. I went up to her and said, "The school got a phone message for you. Here it is."

This piqued Adry's curiosity about me. I handed her the message, and as she unfolded the paper, she said, "Do I know you?"

I glanced over the note as she read it, and she crumpled it up and threw it on the floor.

One by one, each of us was called to go onstage and play our piece. The order was alphabetical, which made this the one time in my life when I was happy to be a Zervakis. I never got to go on at all. Adry went out when it was time for the G's, as you would expect. I was watching from the side of the stage as she walked over to the piano, very quickly. She dropped her music down, flat on the lid of the piano instead of opening it up on the rack—just plopped it down, sat on the piano bench and started to play.

She was pretty fired up. I'm not sure what she was playing, but it wasn't Brahms. It was like nothing I ever heard. Weird music—fantastic . . . but *weeeeird.* The teachers and parents in the theater started muttering to each other, and the rest of the students backstage were gathering around me to watch from the wings.

It didn't take long for Mr. Wundt to march out to the piano. He smiled a ridiculous plastic smile, glared at Adry like he was trying to burn her with his heat-ray vision, and he propped her music up neatly and opened it up. He bowed at the audience, gave Adry another heat-ray-vision glare, and went offstage, walking sideways so he could keep staring at her. Adry never stopped playing the whole time. She just watched Mr. Wundt go through his routine, and she played what she wanted to play.

A bunch of people in the audience applauded when Wundt walked offstage. For a minute, I didn't know if they were clapping for what he did or the fact that he was gone. But it was clear soon enough that a lot of the people—all of the students, definitely—were loving Adry. There were "ooh" and "aaah" sounds, and not another sound in the hall other than Adry's wild music, which just kept getting wilder. Somebody in the Juilliard administration got to the light board and started flicking the stage lights on and off, and that sent Adry off on a tear, playing crazier than ever. People in the audience were clapping for her while she was playing, and that was egging her on. She was bobbing and swaying at the piano, throwing her head back and spinning her hair around as she played. People kept clapping. Finally, somebody in the Juilliard brass had enough, and the stage went black.

People kept applauding and applauding, but Adry wasn't playing anymore. The lights came back up, and she was slumped over the piano, unconscious.

CHAPTER 4

Psychosynesthesia

(1978)

Carolyn Geffel:

I never dreamed that my first trip to New York City would be to see my own daughter in the hospital. I had numerous opportunities to see the Big Apple over the years before that day—they just never panned out. The class of 1954 in our school made a big end-of-the-year trip to New York and saw a Broadway show and went to one of the museums, everything. It was *Pajama Game*, which I eventually saw when they made the movie and absolutely adored. I *love* movie musicals, even when they're on the stage. I've often wondered how different things would be if Adry had gone into that type of music instead of whatever term you would use for what she used to do and, I say, could very well still be doing today. But I was in the class of '55, and we didn't go to New York that year. I think we went to Hershey Park. I can't remember. It's not important.

We got the phone call from the Juilliard School that Adry had been brought to the hospital, which was not a call I was expecting. I don't know if you've ever had a daughter at Juilliard who was suddenly hospitalized, but this was the first time for me, and it was frightening. We turned the business over to Donny for the day and headed for New York. It was nearly closing time, anyway—how much damage could he do? Greg did the driving, and I navigated. I have no problem driving, even on the highway, but we were in a hurry, and if we got pulled over for speeding, Greg is a smoother talker. That's why he excels at the sales in our business, and I take care of the books or, if we're in the car like we were that time, the maps.

It took us ten hours to get to New York, driving straight though all the way without a stop, except for dinner at the Howard Johnson's in New Jersey. When we finally got to the hospital, it was the middle of the night, and you'd never know it. The streets were full of cars and all kinds of people—I mean *all kinds* of people. I looked around, and I realized we could get all the entertainment we wanted on the New York City streets. It didn't matter if we had time to see a Broadway show while we were there.

The hospital Adry was in was called Saint Clare's. I couldn't tell you if it was founded by Saint Clare or named for her after she died or what, exactly. We were told it was close to the Juilliard School, thank goodness for Adry. When we got to her room, she was fast asleep, resting peacefully. We made our way up close to her in her bed, I gave her a kiss on the forehead, and Greg held her by the shoulders and shook her—"Adry! Wake up! What's going on?"

A nurse ran in and quietly grabbed us and pulled us out into the hall. She was a nun—I should say, a combination nurse and nun. I was very impressed. She took us aside and gave us the whole rundown on Adry. She explained how Adry had been playing piano in a concert at the school—*my daughter Adry, playing in a concert!*—and went into some kind of *state* and collapsed. She said the school called an ambulance, and Adry was brought to the hospital unconscious, accompanied by a friend of hers, a boy.

Greg said, "A *boy*? Doesn't sound like our Adry." I gave him a smack on his arm, and we went to the waiting room and sat there for a few hours till it was morning and we were allowed to go back in Adry's room and see her.

Gregory Geffel:

Like any good father, I recognized that I bore some responsibility for my daughter's welfare until she turned twenty-one. I took that responsibility as seriously as possible, as you can tell by the fact I brought her mother in to New York City after work on the first day we learned about her hospitalization. My wife Carolyn had very little in the way of information about this. We weren't privy to the details until we arrived at the hospital. We learned at that juncture that Adrianne was having a mental issue, and she was being examined for that. I was greatly relieved to learn this but hardly shocked. I had suspected all along that there was nothing wrong with her.

Donald Geffel:

I didn't go to New York that time, or ever. I stayed and ran the whole business by myself—no problem.

[Geffel provides details on the operations of the business in his parents' absence.]

Carolyn Geffel:

When we came back to Adry's room, she was awake and sitting up, humming some kind of song to herself. Greg and I couldn't help but laugh. That was our Adry, silly as ever! I gave her a big your-mamma-still-loves-you hug and sat on her bed with her to see how she was feeling, while Greg went to find the cafeteria to get himself some breakfast. We had a very nice talk—she told me about how she had been playing the piano one minute, and the next minute she was here, and I caught her up on all things Greg and I had been doing at home since she moved away. After a time, one of the doctors came in. I don't know if he was a priest, also, or just a doctor. He said they were going to keep Adry in the hospital for a little while for further observation, and I was very, very happy to hear that. If all they were going to do was observe her, I knew she couldn't be a very sick girl.

Greg and I thought we might as well stay in New York another day and went over to Juilliard to see about using one of the free rooms they had for overnight visits like when Adry and her friend Barb Lucher stayed over at the school. We had a terrible time getting any information about that and finally gave up. We made the drive home after lunch, with me in the navigator's seat again.

Dr. Emil Vanderlinde (former director, Neurological Institute of New York):

I was brought in on this case by the head of neurology at Saint Clare's Hospital at the point when it became apparent to the team at that facility that they were in way over their heads. The Neurological Institute of New York, which I was part of but not yet heading up, was directly affiliated with the Columbia University Medical Center, which had no relationship with Saint Clare's. From time to time, nonetheless, I would be contacted by various institutions throughout the New York area on cases of special interest such as this.

Adrianne Geffel was the first patient to suffer from psychosynesthesia that I would encounter, and I am nearly certain hers was the first case to be documented in North America. This is not to suggest that no human being had ever shown symptoms of psychosynesthesia prior to Geffel. Retroactive analysis suggests that it may have been present to certain degrees in several historical figures of note, including the composer Charles Ives and the jazz musician John Coltrane. Multiple cases have been identified and treated successfully, or less successfully, in the years following Geffel. Still, her case is viewed as a landmark in the neurological literature.

I have written rather extensively on this subject, as you surely know. Indeed, it was my work on Geffel's case of psychosynesthesia that led to my being awarded the Vicary Prize in Neuroscience in 1986. I subsequently earmarked a portion of the monetary benefit to underwrite a reward for information on Geffel's whereabouts, which is still in effect.

I believe I can explain psychosynesthesia for you in lay terms. Allow me to try.

It has long been known that in normal brains there is a strong connection between the auditory system and the limbic system. The input from the auditory system stimulates the auditory cortex in the temporal lobe. In so-called normal people, there's a strong connection between the auditory cortex and parts of the limbic system such as the amygdala and the hypothalamus. This is why many people often have strong emotional reactions to music. Music elicits activity in the amygdala and stirs emotions such as joy or sadness or even anxiety. In addition, there are connections that go both ways—not only from the auditory cortex to the amygdala, but also from the amygdala back to the auditory cortex. With psychosynesthesia, there is an exceptionally strong connection from the amygdala and the hippocampus back to the auditory cortex, so that when the patients are experiencing strong emotions, they receive input back to the auditory cortex. Patients experience this as hearing music in their minds.

When I first examined Adrianne Geffel, it was clear that there was a powerful connection between the limbic system and the auditory system, but we didn't fully understand exactly how those connections were made and exactly what parts of the limbic system were involved. Since then, through neuroscience research with animal models and through magnetic resonance imaging studies, we have identified which parts of the brain are actually involved in this circuit. So, for example, we now know that there's a thalamus-amygdala-colliculus feedback circuit that makes connections and triggers responses when listening to music. Also, we know that the superficial amygdala is more sensitive to pleasant or joyful music, and the lateral basal amygdala is more sensitive to sad music.

In a sense, what the psychosynesthesia patient experiences are auditory hallucinations, in that the patient is hearing music that others around them do not hear. It's similar to the way that other auditory hallucinations occur. Auditory hallucinations—particularly musical hallucinations—can, for example, accompany alcohol withdrawal at times. In Adrianne Geffel, there was not an episodic event that occurred during particular disturbances. The hallucinations were virtually continuous. She heard music almost all the time. It was the flavor of the music that changed, along with the intensity, in direct relation to her emotional state. Over the course of her life, she learned to live with the fact that she was almost always hearing music and, in fact, found a way to release what she was experiencing by playing the music on the piano.

Since she was hearing music in her head, when she would hear other music from an outside source, it would produce a dissonance, because the music was not compatible. There was no consonance to music she was experiencing independently and the music from the external input. That activates the amygdala to trigger anxiety and fear reactions. Also, since she is almost continuously experiencing music, there is a strong connection to the hypothalamus, and the hypothalamus can trigger release of hormones and also affects regulation of the parasympathetic nervous system and affects the regulation of the heart rate. The result would have a pronounced amplification of her emotions. For example, if she were feeling distressed and were hearing distressing music, this would have a feedback effect to make her more distressed. This could affect her physiology through the release of hormones, increased EMP and ephrins in the body, and so forth.

You can find a more detailed explanation and analysis of psychosynesthesia as a neurological condition and Adrianne Geffel's case in particular in my book *She Heard Music but There Was No Instrument There: How America's Top Neurologist Changed Adrianne Geffel's Life*. If you'd like a copy, I can help arrange for you to order one through my office.

Ann Athema (conceptual artist):

Geffel was sublime. Honestly, the sublimest. We did quite a lot together. Strange to think we met in the hospital, but I guess it makes some kind of sense—wouldn't you say? We were the two arty ones. That's how they pegged us. Actually, though, I wasn't making art anymore. I gave it up, and that's why I was there. And that's how I met Geffel.

We met in the art room. [Athema refers to the space designated for Creative Therapy at the Neurological Institute of New York.] I was there first, and Geffel arrived there later. She was transferred from another facility [Saint Clare's Hospital]. I'm a few years older than she. I was out of school by that time. I went to Cooper Union and then, right out of school, I was chosen to be in a group show. Fantastic, and then I looked at what everybody was doing, and I honestly couldn't see any point in painting anymore. *Everybody* was doing *everything*. There was nothing left for me to do. So I gave it up. I just stopped painting. I really didn't see any reason to do it anymore. To tell you the truth, I didn't feel like doing much of anything. I didn't go outside. I didn't eat. One day, my parents came into town to visit. They went to my apartment down on Ludlow Street, and I suppose I didn't answer the buzzer. They got the super to let them in, and they brought me to NYU hospital, and from there I was sent up to the institute. A little while after that, Geffel arrived.

Somebody must have said, "She's an artist" or "She acts like an artist," so they kept bringing me to the art room and setting up a canvas on an easel in front of me. I'd just look at it for a while and never touch the paint brushes. At one point, someone came along and asked me how I was doing, and I said, "I've completed that artwork. Could you bring me another canvas?" I never picked up a brush. They came back with a fresh canvas, and I put the first one on the floor and propped the new one up on the easel. I glanced at it but never touched it, and someone came around again and looked at the two blank canvases and asked me how I felt about what I was doing.

I said, "I have two works finished now. I'm quite pleased with them both." I pointed to the blank canvas on the floor, and I said, "That one is a portrait of God—not as conceived in the image of man, but a precise, literal depiction."

I turned to the canvas on the easel and said, "And this is a more personal work, a composite portrait of every woman I have descended from, since the dawn of humanity. I think they're both rather vivid, don't you? I'd like to continue my art, if you'd be so kind as to bring me more canvases." A little while later, someone came out with half a dozen new canvases and laid them down in a pile next to the unopened paints.

The next day, same thing. Before long, I had a nice stack of blank canvases that I announced to be completed artworks. They'd ask me, "And what have you done today?" And I'd say, "Oh—so much! Look—that one shows the known universe, in actual size. And the other one is the unknown universe." They all thought I was serious. It was hysterical.

There was a piano in the corner, and Geffel would be there playing her heart away. She was extraordinary. Not that easy for me to follow, but *extraordinary*.

One day, she walked over to me to see what I had been doing. I said, "Would you care to see my artwork?" and I went through my whole pile of blank canvases, which was pretty high by now. I picked up each one very slowly and carefully and held it up for her to see. I said, "This, as you can see, is a pack of timber wolves enacting the murder of Hypatia in ballet, adorned in period costume. I think you'll like the next one in particular. This is your music, embodied as ice sculpture, melted, evaporated, crystallized, and dissipated in the air that feeds the breath of sparrows and mice."

When I was finished, I looked at her straight-faced. Geffel studied the canvases and said, "I *love* these. This is the most ridiculous art I've ever seen, and the most wonderful." I burst out laughing, and Geffel gave me a funny little smile. But she kept looking at the canvases.

Biran Zervakis:

I could barely grasp that my dear, precious Adry was alone, without me, in the sterile environs of a hospital. I was at her side after she passed out, of course. I accompanied the emergency team that brought her to the hospital, and visited her the very next day that I was free. The poor girl was so disoriented she looked surprised to see me. And yet, for all she was going through, she was still interested in *me*. I walked into her room and took a seat in the chair by her bed. Adry peered over at me, and she said, "What's your *story*?"

I talked to her for some time as she rested with her eyes closed, I'm fairly sure, though I couldn't see her face from the way she was lying. Not wanting to tax her, I left after a couple of hours, when a helpful security guard guided me to the exit.

When I returned to school, I filled in all our classmates and the teachers on Adry's status. I told them not to worry, I would be checking on her and reporting back regularly. I made the acquaintance of quite a few students I hadn't had the occasion to meet before. One of the most fruitful of these new connections was with Sue Takashima, who followed in her father's lead and went to work for the Sony Corporation, in the field of recorded music, after graduation. When I introduced myself to Sue and we started talking about Adry, she told me her father also happened to have an interest in Adry, because he had alerted someone at Sony to the way Adry loved to listen to cassettes with headphones, and they were developing a product based on the concept. I found this fascinating.

Barbara Lucher:

I'm not going to talk about this. I wasn't there. I couldn't be there. I didn't even know she was *in* the fucking hospital. Nobody told me.

Ask me something else. Ask me why her parents didn't have the common courtesy to pick up the god-damn fucking telephone and tell their daughter's best friend that she was in the fucking hospital. I have a thought or two about that. Ask me why my witch aunt Connie took her car from me just when I really could have used it, if only somebody had the decency to alert me to the fact that Adry was in the hospital and might have liked a visit from me. Ask me *that*.

[Lucher is asked those questions.]

Fuck you, Mr. Clever Man. *Fuck you*.

[Lucher is asked why she thinks Adrianne Geffel's parents failed to inform her of Adrianne Geffel's hospitalization.]

Have you ever been in love, Mr. Clever Man? Do you think it *showed*? Could other people *tell*? Did they all jump up and down and cheer you on? Maybe they did, for you and your lucky love. Maybe you can tell me all about that. I'm not very familiar with that.

Dr. Emil Vanderlinde:

Adrianne Geffel was under observation at the Neurological Institute for ten days. We had no treatment protocol for psychosynesthesia at the time. We did all we could do, and provided her with what could be described as an approximation of musical therapy. We gave her access to a piano to play.

Music therapy was still a young field at the time of Adrianne Geffel's diagnosis. It was as much a form of recreation or a break from treatment as it was an instrument of treatment itself. In the Geffel case, however, music played a central role in the disorder and a commensurate role in its treatment. During the time she was under our care at the institute, Adrianne made considerable progress through the playing of music. We had the benefit of input from an educator at New York University, Professor Ruth LeMat, who had been working with the patient informally. Through Professor LeMat, we were able to successfully achieve a level of intellectual understanding, distinct from a subjective appreciation, of the music Adrianne Geffel produced in the act of channelling the auditory hallucinations she experienced. Professor LeMat gave us every reason to accept that Adrianne's music was *good*. We could see directly that making it was good *for her*.

Since the character of the music had a direct correlation to her emotional state at the time she was creating it, the music provided unfiltered evidence of the progress of her care. I can show you what I mean. I had my staff pull my file on this. I thought you would find it interesting. [Vanderlinde calls for an assistant, and the assistant hands him a folder containing a medical log, which Vanderlinde flips through until he finds a page with a Post-it note attached.] Here—May 21:

> Patient brought to rec center. Gravitated quickly to piano. Music unusual, abrasive. Unclear if she is purposely playing badly—aggression to care-givers?—or is incompetent. Latter unlikely—Juilliard student. Possible Lincoln Center donor family—check this. Drove other patients from room. Complaints from staff.

In the margins there, I have a little note, too:

> See about buying electric organ—volume control?

Four days later, May 25:

> Patient acclimating to new environment. Appears less agitated, some music played less hostile. Almost enjoyable.

And four days after that, May 29:

> Prepare to discharge. Normal functionality at most times. Arrange for follow-up, ongoing study of P-S [psychosynesthesia]. Important case—share findings. Book deal?

Ann Athema:

Geffel didn't get a lot of visitors—a woman who was her teacher, she told me, and that Biran person came by every couple of days and talked at her while she played the piano. Her family was from the Midwest or somewhere distant and didn't visit. I had a sister and a couple of friends from Cooper Union who came to see me, and a guy, Jeffy, who I had been seeing now and then, came quite a bit. Geffel kept playing the piano, and I kept not painting. And we'd talk. If somebody came to visit me, Geffel would sit with us. Sometimes, I'd get her to play something for us. She'd say, "Alright, Koshka—you asked for it."

Before they released me, one of the artists from the group show I had done came to visit—Armutt Canterell. His real name was Armond, but he signed his paintings Armutt—like R. Mutt, Duchamp's *non de plume*. I *know*. But—listen, it was the Seventies. He came by, and I showed him my complete collection of untouched canvases. I said, "Armutt—I think a person with your highly developed sensibility would appreciate this work." One by one, I showed him the canvases and explained what each of them was. I looked him in the eye and said, "You understand what I have achieved here, don't you, Armutt?" I never cracked a smile, and Armutt nodded solemnly.

The next day, he came back with the dealer from the K. Lewitt Gallery, where our group show had been. He looked over all the canvases, one at a time, as I explained them—"This is avarice and charity, locked in the eternal battle for the human heart, and this is every mother's son and every father's daughter, ever, in group therapy." Geffel was playing her music in the corner. He said, "I'd like to show these. Would you be interested in having a show of your own at K. Lewitt?"

I said, "Perhaps. But the music you're hearing is integral to my concept. That's the great avant-garde composer Adrianne Geffel over there. Can you bring a piano into the gallery?"

CHAPTER 5

A Geyser on Grand Street

(1978–1979)

Sandor Kalman (former chief curator, K. Lewitt Gallery):

I knew Adrianne Geffel very well, of course. I discovered her. This is well known. I discovered many of the artists and also the musicians. Richard Prince, I discovered. Chuck Close, Steve Reich, Richard Serra—they were workers in a moving company when I discovered them. They had a truck. They carried boxes and furniture—whatever you needed moved, they moved it. That's what they did. No one knew they were artistic. Chuck Close, an *artist*? Steve Reich, a *musician*? They were *movers*, and then I discovered them. They moved all the furnishings from our original location on 135 Crosby Street to our much better space at 82 Spring Street. They did very good work for me for a very nice price, and I recommended them to everyone. Before that, no one ever heard their names.

I discovered them all: Robert Smithson, Cindy Sherman, Chris Burden—Jeff Koons, of course—we are very good friends. I gave them their start, I gave them money, so they would have a few dollars while the accountant worked on the books. That could take a very long time, and there was not always much money left for the artist. I took care of them out of my own pocket. Many times, I gave them ideas for their art. Artists don't like to talk about that. That's fine—I don't do what I do for recognition. I'm satisfied with the commissions. But it's not always what it looks like.

Chris Burden, I never got along with. I wanted to shoot him, but I didn't have a gun. And what did he do? He went ahead and found someone with a gun, and asked him to shoot him. The man missed. He just got a little of his arm. But he used my concept.

Adrianne Geffel, I introduced to the world. I gave Adrianne Geffel her premiere at my gallery, with the artist Ann Athema. I gave Ann Athema her first solo show at the same time. So many things, I started. So many more I could have started, but somebody did them first.

And that's all I can tell you about Adrianne Geffel. She was very grateful to me. She admired me very much. For that alone, you could say she was not unusual. But I was very happy to have the opportunity to introduce her. That led to so many things over the years, and now this book. It's amazing to think—you and I would not be having this conversation right now, if I weren't here with you.

[Kalman is asked to recount how he came to present Adrianne Geffel in a gallery setting.]

I remember, I first got the idea to put music in a gallery after seeing Steve Reich perform in a gallery. That's how the concept came to me. Ann Athema was happy with the idea to have Adrianne Geffel play at her show. We had no piano, of course—it was an art gallery. It wasn't the Copacabana. So we used an electric keyboard that Reich brought for us to use. He charged us only for the moving.

Ann Athema:

Armutt, because he changed his name, thought I should change my name, too. Armutt thought everyone should find a new name and become a new person. He would say, "In the future, everybody is going to change their identity every fifteen minutes." I said, "I see, and now you're Andy Warhol. In fifteen minutes, could you please become someone more original?"

Armutt came up with the name Ann Athema for me. Like "anathema"—get it? Hardee-har-har-har. Armutt was the great avant-garde punster. There was a fellow named Bob Sheff around then—he was a Texan and played blues piano in a bar band. Armutt renamed him Gene Tyranny—T-Y-R-A-N-N-Y—and he became a *thing.* Armutt was trying to find somebody to call Kurt Vile—V-I-L-E—but no one went along with it, because they didn't get the reference. Years later, I saw that a singer was going by the name Kurt Vile, but it turned out that Kurt Vile was the guy's real name. Armutt was *furious.*

I liked becoming Ann Athema, actually—it was ludicrous. I thought of going with Irma Neutica, but Armutt was working with a drag artist he was grooming to call Irma La Douche, so Irma was taken. Working in public under the guise of Ann Athema allowed me to function without creative pressure, protected by the armor of irony.

Geffel was a different creature entirely. I was a nest of insecurities and anxieties hiding behind a joke name, making joke art. Geffel was pure truth and openness. Her emotions were her music, and her music was absolute emotion. I never experienced anything like that.

We arranged for Geffel to play at the opening of my show at K. Lewitt, and she ended up playing at the gallery every night for a month or more, I believe. I thought she would be a good fit, because the whole idea of art and music then was to do things that didn't fit together. Trisha Brown was walking up the side of the building in an alley down the street. Larry Rivers was painting while he was playing the saxophone and making a plaster cast of his dick at the same time. *No*, if you want to know—I wasn't there to see that, luckily. But I do know people who have seen the plaster cast, and a lot more people who have seen the dick.

I told the gallery I wanted no canvases on the walls at all. I would describe the art, and that would *be* the art. The gallery people were ecstatic, in the diffident and alienating way gallery people experienced ecstasy, and I saved a lot of money on canvases. Before the doors opened, Geffel paced around the gallery, looking over the empty walls, humming to herself. She said to me, "I hope you know, Koshka, I can't promise to match the *spirit* of your artwork."

I said, "I know, Geffel—I've heard you play. That's why you're here."

She made that odd little smile of hers, and she said, "Hey, Koshka—thanks."

The opening of the show was fairly well attended. There were twenty or twenty-five people there—all the people who went to every opening, to ogle one another and be seen by one another. The director of the gallery introduced me, and I walked slowly all the way around the room and pointed to empty spaces on the walls. I said, "This is one of the earliest pieces in this series. It is the secret of life, pretending to be the secret of death." I gazed at the wall for a moment and walked a few feet, and I said, "This is the earliest childhood memories of everyone here tonight superimposed over the worst fears of everyone coming here tomorrow."

When I had covered all the wall space, I thanked people for coming and told them to enjoy the art while they listened to the music of an important new composer. I introduced Geffel, and she started playing a little electric keyboard the gallery rented from Steve Reich. Within a few minutes, everyone in the galley had gathered around her, watching her and listening intently.

Geffel was terribly nervous, and that only made the music more . . . like Geffel's music.

Jon Geldman (music critic):

If you've read any of my writing on Adrianne Geffel, you know I rank her among the most important musical artists I've ever deemed to be worthy of my consideration. I wrote about her frequently from the time of her debut at the K. Lewitt Gallery to the night at Weill Hall at the end of her career. You'd be interested to know I'm in the process of collecting the pieces for an anthology of my work on Geffel and her music. It will be titled *Geldman on Geffel* or, potentially, *Geffel by Geldman*—which do you like better? Tell me.

[Geldman is told each title has its attributes.]

I agree with you—they're both so good, I'm sure I'd do well with either one. I can't give you the publisher at the moment, because I don't have a contract for the book signed at this stage. But I'd be happy to show you the manuscript—I brought a copy for you. I know you'd find it informative.

You've never seen Adrianne Geffel perform yourself, have you? You said in your email that you've never met her. I find that curious and sad. You'll learn a lot from my writing. I'll share it with you, and you may want to pass it along to the publisher of the book you're trying to do. I'll give you the name and contact information for my literary agent, as well, when I have that lined up.

The first time I saw Adrianne Geffel perform was practically the first time anyone saw her, just one day after the opening of the gallery show with Ann Athema. I was writing for the *SoHo Weekly News* as a freelancer. There was no staff to speak of and very little money—just the privilege of writing for countless dozens of other moneyless lovers of art and music, ideas and sex of every variety, including new varieties being invented on the spot. The atmosphere was utterly free—everything was free, thank God, because we were all impoverished. But bountiful in creative thought and over-stuffed with excitement about the expanding world of the arts and our role in it.

I was friends of a sort with the art critic for the paper, Julian Hough, and he reviewed the art show of Ann Athema's. He liked the artwork, to the extent that Julian liked any art. If you've read the review he wrote, it was Julian who coined the term Athematics for the work. The day after the opening, I bumped into Julian at the *SoHo News* office. I was there for a few hours, waiting for a check for a review I had done several months earlier, and Julian came in to hand in a piece. He said, "Oh, Jon—I saw a show last night at K. Lewitt. The artwork was somewhat interesting. It's neo-conceptual and post-minimalist. The art world will be calling it Athematics. There was music, as well."

I said, "Is the music neo-conceptual, too? Because I'm really not much of a *neo* person. I'm far more *proto*." Julian thought I was being serious, and I probably did, too. We were all so *seriously* serious.

Julian said, "That's not a bad question," which is what Julian would say to let you know he thinks it's a *terrible* question. *It's not bad—it's terrible.*

I said, "Well, if the music is truly post-minimalist, I like it already." I had heard quite a lot of minimalist music at that point, and I was more than ready for the *post*. I was up for a little maximalism, and that's exactly what I found when I arrived at the K. Lewitt.

I went on the first day I heard about her, on the second night of the show. When I walked in, there was a group of people standing all around Adrianne Geffel while she played. I had to jostle my way through the crowd to get to the front, so I could see what Geffel was doing—"Excuse me, *SoHo News*—I need to get through—*SoHo News* . . ." I was not above flaunting my credentials. I got just a foot from the keyboard, to Geffel's side—on her right, which I did strategically in order to observe how she employed the upper registers—and I didn't move until her time was up, an hour and a half later and Sandor Kalman had the keyboard unplugged. I don't think I *breathed* for an hour and a half, and it didn't appear as if Adrianne Geffel took a single breath, either. Every so often, she would begin to quiet down for a moment—it felt as if she were winding up her musical thoughts, and everyone would applaud, and, instantly, that would rev her up again. I know you've never seen her, so I doubt you can fully grasp her artistry, unless you've read my writing on the subject.

I can read you an excerpt from the essay I wrote about that evening. It was published in the next issue of the *SoHo News*, though in the visual-art section, because Geffel was appearing in a gallery. Julian Hough complained that I got space that he should have gotten to cover art, but I held my tongue. Why be petty?

I'll read you a bit of the text. This is the documentation of what

I experienced that night, as I wrote it—expanded and revised for inclusion in my collection:

> I have seen the future of the avant-garde, and her name is Adrianne Geffel.
>
> One day, I'll look back on this review and marvel at my good fortune for being the first critic to hear, to appreciate, and to acknowledge Adrianne Geffel for the potency and originality of her art. I witnessed her performance last night at the K. Lewitt Gallery, where she is appearing, ostensibly, to provide an aural counterpart to the neo-conceptual art of Ann Athema.
>
> Adrianne Geffel's music offers not merely aural counterpoint to the so-called "Athematics" of Athema's canvases, but dramatic contrast to it. It is robustly emotional and emotionally robust, assaultively combustive and combustively assaultive, thoroughly great and greatly thorough.
>
> It will no doubt take this critic years to come fully to terms with Geffel's heterodox art, as I witness future performances that I could never imagine now. Readers interested in how musical art evolves and how that evolution can earn its due recognition, with that very evolution facilitated by critical nurturing, will be intrigued to read future pieces by me on Adrianne Geffel's music, as I come to write them.

Shall I go on? It's just about two thousand words, with the material I've added.

[Gelman is told that a printed version of the article would be sufficient.]

I see. Well, I'll send you a copy of it, with the rest of the text to my book. You and your publisher will find it well worth reading, and publishing.

Milijenko Jervic (longtime loft owner/host):

Call me Milo, please. Why be formal? Life is too short! When a man calls me Mr. Jervic, I know he is an attorney or an accountant, and we won't be having a lot of fun together. All my friends call me Milo. Let's be friends!

I would like to tell you but I cannot recall if I read an article about Adrianne Geffel first and then I heard her play the piano or if Darius read me an article about her out loud to me first and then I heard her play. Darius enjoyed reading to me, and I enjoyed listening to him read. He was a beautiful reader and beautiful in every way. He loved Adrianne Geffel! We went to hear her together at the K. Lewitt Gallery, and we could not believe what we were hearing. Ooooh . . . *the best!*

I said to him, "Darius, what is this music? I don't understand." He said, "Milo . . . who cares? What does that matter? She is a *phenomenon*. We must have her to our loft!" And so we invited her to come to our loft and play, and that was the beginning of the very famous Adrianne Geffel concerts in my loft.

Adrianne loved to play my piano. I have a very wonderful Bösendorfer grand piano that I purchased to decorate the loft when I bought it in 1974. As you can see—look around us—the space is very large. I need things that are beautiful and very big to fill it.

[Jervic rises from his chair and walks to the far side of the loft to point out the piano.]

Before I bought the building, this floor was a factory for making zippers. It was out of business by the time I bought it. I rented the two floors below us to artists, and I moved in here, and this is where I had the famous parties. We didn't use the piano for the first ones. I used my very fine stereo system from Germany. I told people, "Can you believe, this used to be a zipper factory?" They said, "Milo, there's more noise from zippers here tonight than there was in the factory!" It was true! *The best!*

Then, Darius moved in here, and he knew all the painters and sculptors and musicians and intellectuals. They all came to the parties. The musicians loved my Bösendorfer. The intellectuals loved the musicians. The musicians invited other musicians, and the parties became concerts. People came just to hear the music, and for the drugs. Darius knew everything about all the latest drugs, and enjoyed trying them and sharing them. All the most wonderful musicians were here, and they played for each other. I don't know all their names—Darius would be able to tell you every name. But he's been gone for eleven years. We loved each other very much. He also loved the drugs, too-too much.

The concerts were so wonderful—*the best!* Everybody listened very carefully. You would not hear the sound of a single zipper. A documentary film was made about music in SoHo during this time, and the producer came here to shoot and interview me. He told me, "Mr. Jervic, do you know you are the father of the SoHo loft-music scene?" I said, "No, no—call me Milo!" He photographed my piano, with no one playing it. He asked me, "Is this the same piano that Adrianne Geffel played? Was it right here in this spot when she played it? What was she like?"

I will tell you what I told him. Adrianne Geffel was beautiful! She was like magic! Her music, I never cared for—I don't understand what that was that she was playing. But I knew it was very serious. Everyone told me. But *Adrianne*—she was magnificent. She was a very pretty girl—not a fancy person, but beautiful and strong, like a peasant girl from my country [Estonia]. I saw girls in my country who were barely not children anymore but lived with death and sacrifice, and they would sit quietly by themselves. That was Adrianne Geffel.

I don't know how many concerts she gave here—thirty, forty, probably more in those two or three years. The first time, she was nobody—she played a little toy organ in the K. Lewitt Gallery, that was it. By the end, she was a celebrity.

If you ask me, "Milo, what happened to her?" I will tell you, she changed. The last time I saw her, she played at The Kitchen, down the street from where we are. She played the most beautiful music I ever heard a person play. I can tell you, for the first time I enjoyed Adrianne's music. That was the last time I ever saw her.

Bobby Akbar-Aleem (soprano saxophonist):

I was blessed to witness her on multiple occasions in one loft or another. Her music was deeply felt by all. I created with her in various lofts and such settings of mental openness to the art. She inspired me to find the feeling within myself and give voice to it in the music.

[Akbar-Aleem is asked to describe their approach to collaboration.]

We created in the same time and space, if you choose to categorize that as collaboration. I drew inspiration from the truth in her music, and I attempted to bring my own truth to the experience.

[Akbar-Aleem is asked to describe how Geffel responded to his contributions as a collaborator.]

We were united on the plane of emotion. We did not concern ourselves with the technicalities of musical structures or notes. We did not listen to one another in the historical sense. I had awareness that the sound of my instrument appeared to disturb her. This was her truth. My truth was mine.

Ann Athema:

The K. Lewitt show was over, and I went back to not doing art, but Geffel was playing music every night. I went to a fair number of the loft concerts, and they were even more disorienting than they sounded on the recordings people started making. You've heard those records. Geffel was *erupting*. I was beyond excited for her, but I was seriously concerned about her, too.

She stayed in my place on Ludlow Street sometimes when the concert was over, instead of going all the way up to her room uptown. She crashed on my couch. We hung out and went for coffee and biscotti at Dimicci's. Sometimes, my boyfriend Jeffy came with us, if he stayed over at my place—we all got along, because he worked on the signal grid for the MTA [Metropolitan Transit Authority] and didn't try to act like he knew more about art and music than Geffel and I did. At the MTA, he was used to not understanding what was happening. The best memory I have from those days is one day on a Sunday afternoon, we were walking around on the Lower East Side, deciding on where to go for coffee and talking, just the two of us. Geffel said, "You know, Koshka, there's something weird about these concerts I'm giving."

I said, "I know, Geffel—it's called your music. I've heard it."

She gave me a scrunched-up-face dirty look, and she said, "That's not what I'm talking about. I mean, it's weird for me to do." She said, "I'm a nervous wreck when I'm doing it, and that only seems to make it more successful. I feel awful, and so I make awful-sounding music. But it feels weirdly good to do that. I'm not sure how to explain it."

A while later, we're still walking around—now we're on Norfolk Street or Stanton Street—and as we're walking, we see a homeless man in front of us, pacing around in a circle on the sidewalk. We slow down when we get close to him, and Geffel reaches in her handbag for her wallet, to give him some money. He stares at us and starts screaming, "Fuck cunt! Fuck! Fuck cunt! Fuck! Fuck!"

Geffel tosses a dollar on the sidewalk, and I yank her across the street. We keep walking, but a lot faster now. We get to the street corner. We're waiting for the light to change, and some guy barges into me from behind me to get ahead of us to cross the street. He practically knocks me over, but he doesn't say "Excuse me" or anything—he just plants himself right in front of us and rushes ahead when the light changes. Geffel gives me a jab with her elbow and says, "Go ahead—try it," and I scream at the top of my lungs, "Fuck cunt! Fuck! Fuck cunt!"

I look over at Geffel, and she's watching me and giving me that smile of hers. She says, "I told you. It's weird, isn't it?"

Jeffrey Knudsen (former boyfriend of Ann Athema):

I was going with Ann Athema. We started to get serious, and we moved in together after a few months. I met her—when I met her, she was still going by her real name, which was Valerie Koshka. I called her Val—or Vallie and sometimes, [when it was] just the two of us, Vallie Girl, because she was anything but. She was very close to Adry Geffel—closer than I was, but I knew her. I liked her. I never really appreciated her music, until the late stuff. But I liked her, better than I liked her music.

Biran Zervakis:

And now for the tale of our reunion in SoHo. I was tingling with joy when I spotted an article about Adry in the *SoHo Weekly News*, posted on the bulletin board in the lounge at Juilliard. There was a four-column headline—"A Geyser on Grand Street"—and a nice but much, much too small photo of Adry playing a very grand grand piano. I said to myself, *Of course my Adry is being written up in the premier journal of avant-garde art in New York!* I knew the most astute enthusiasts of contemporary music would appreciate Adry and her music the way I did.

Since we hadn't seen each other in several weeks, I assumed she left town and moved back home with her parents after her hospitalization. I wanted desperately to see her, mainly to see her beatific face again, and secondarily to present her with her share of the funds I had arranged to procure on her behalf from Sony. With the aid of a team of my parents' attorneys, I had filed a notice of intent to litigate over Sony's unauthorized use of Adry's concept of a personal sound system using cassettes and headphones. Not to bother her with the legalistic mechanics, I instructed the attorneys to reach a settlement. We agreed to accept a buy-out of fifty thousand dollars, paid to the order of a limited-liability partnership I had set up for the purpose. I couldn't wait to see Adry, break this excellent news to her, and bestow her with a payment of forty-one thousand dollars for her share of the buyout, after my commission of fifteen percent and expenses.

I saw in the *SoHo News* that Adry would be giving a loft concert on Grand Street that Saturday night, and I went to see her with a sixty-dollar bouquet of long-stemmed red roses in one hand and a check for forty thousand nine hundred forty dollars in the other hand. As soon as Adry saw me, she gave me that look of secret code between us, acting surprised and turning away. She scooted over to the piano and began the concert, which was absolutely exhilarating, naturally. Adry was on fire, as always, positively bursting with music. Once or twice, I caught her eye while she played, and the music would suddenly erupt. I was terribly touched to see I was inspiring her so.

At the end of the concert, people came up to the piano to talk to her. I broke through the crowd and said, "Excuse me, ladies and gentlemen—I have an announcement to make. It's a surprise for Adrianne. My name is Biran Zervakis. B-I-R-A-N, 'Zervakis' as it sounds. I am Adrianne's dear friend and classmate at the Juilliard School of Music. I am pleased to announce that the Sony Corporation of America has officially recognized Adrianne's creative innovations in sound technology." I turned to Adry and laid her check in front of her on the piano, upside down.

I said, "Won't you join me in congratulating Adry with a hearty round of applause?" Everyone started clapping, and I turned to look at Adry as I clapped along. Adry snuck a peek at the check, and quickly slapped it back down on its face.

She rose up and said, "Thank you very much, everybody, for coming to hear me tonight," and she added quietly, just for me,

"I'll talk to you later." She picked the check up from the piano, and left.

I knew she wanted to talk later, but I had trouble finding her after that.

Ruth Sirotta LeMat:

The next time I saw Adrianne, I wasn't expecting her. Having visited her at the Neurological Institute of New York and consulted with Dr. Vanderlinde on her musical ability, I was fully aware of her diagnosis and health status. I had learned from my late husband Pierson that she had taken a medical leave from the Juilliard School. I read a *New York Times* article about the new music in the SoHo lofts, and I was tickled to see Adrianne's name appearing somewhat prominently in that. There were two or three full paragraphs dedicated to Adrianne. It was laudatory in the imperious manner of the *Times'* arts coverage then and now. The point of the article was to recognize the emergence of a variety of young iconoclasts who were averting the strictures of the traditional institutions of presentation to make unorthodox music in the art galleries and lofts of SoHo. The fact that the *New York Times* was acknowledging this phenomenon was important—it meant that this was already old news among musicians.

As an instructor at NYU, I had heard about the musical developments in SoHo—the lofts were literally across the road from the school, on the other side of Houston Street. Several of my composition students had attended some of the loft concerts and experimented with ways to take part in that. It was difficult to do successfully. Adrianne made it appear easier than it was, even for her.

It was a Friday morning at nine or ten o'clock. I was home—few classes were scheduled on Fridays, to help the undergraduates get a head start on their weekend debauchery—and Pierson was out, at a committee meeting at Juilliard. The doorbell rang, and it was Adrianne. We gave each other a warm hug, and I said, "You're a clever one, Adrianne. How did you know I had pound cake?"

We went straight to the dinette and dove in. I told her how happy I was to see her name in the *New York Times* and said I'd love to attend one of her loft concerts. Adrianne said, "I've played through all the Hundred Variations. I'm working on another thousand now." We laughed and munched on the cake.

She said, "Mrs. LeMat, I'd like to ask you something. I don't want to go back to Juilliard."

I said, "That's not a question, Adrianne—that's a statement. It's rare to find someone your age who's so sure of what she wants. I'm impressed. Now, what is it you want to ask me?"

She said, "Oh . . . I forget." She smiled at me, and we had some more cake.

I said, "I trust you're making a little money from playing in the lofts. Just please don't forget, the mind and the body require sustenance that art alone cannot provide. Will your parents be helping you?"

Adrianne said, "That isn't necessary." She explained that she had come into a small windfall recently that she was going to split with a friend from home. That would be enough to get her started, especially if she lived in Greenwich Village, where living expenses were low.

Biran Zervakis:

Adry reached out to me directly, to clear up her confusion over the payout from Sony. My dear Adry, in her understandable excitement over the deal I made for her, hadn't realized the check I gave her at the concert was merely a "show check," for her to frame! It wasn't intended to be actually cashed! When she deposited it and realized that, she got my number from someone at Juilliard, we had a little chat on the phone and made a plan to talk further over coffee in the lounge at the law firm that handled the deal for me. You could say this was our first date, but I've never liked to put labels on anything between Adry and me.

I can't discuss everything involved in that conversation while you're recording us, because the subject of Barb Lucher did come up, and my counsel has advised me against making any public statements about her, owing to some matters currently pending. I personally wouldn't mind answering anything you ask me about Lucher or anything else negative. But you know what lawyers are like!

I can give you the general outline of things. Adry had the idea in her pretty head that Lucher should receive half of her share of the Sony payout. Evidently, she thought she could write Lucher a check on the sum of funds represented for symbolic purposes on that show check. I explained to Adry that I would take care of paying Lucher directly—she didn't have to give that another thought—and I laid out for her how I could help her by managing her share of the Sony payment, cutting any checks she needed, so she would be able to concentrate on her music and not get bogged down with finances. Adry thought about that for a second and said, "I don't like the sound of that."

I assured her, "Nobody knows more than you about the sounds you like and don't like!" I couldn't help but chuckle at my own joke, while she thought about what I said. Then I broke the big news: Through one of my father's operations, I learned about a floor-through loft space on East 3rd Street in Greenwich Village. It was fully furnished and available for immediate occupancy. The rent, for Adry, would be four hundred twenty-five dollars per month—a bit steep, I recognized, but utilities were included, and she wouldn't have to pay a deposit, because I had the inside track on the deal. I had thoughtfully already taken care of signing the lease on her behalf. I thought it best to explain all those details to her another time. I told her she could move in on the first of the month—she didn't have to do a thing but pack her toothbrush.

Adry said, "I'm not sure I like the sound of that, either."

I laughed again and said, "Ah . . . but you'll love the *sight* of it!" I gave her the address and a set of the keys, and I said, "Just check it out tomorrow. If you like it, it's yours!" Only I knew it was hers already! The lease was technically mine, naturally, but it would be hers, because it was mine and, in my heart, I was hers.

CHAPTER 6

Chords and Baffling

(1979–1981)

Ann Athema:

I imagine most of this is in the court records, if the case ever made it that far. Maybe they settled, and that Biran made good on the rent he never paid, or it's still in legal limbo. The way this started was Geffel withdrew from Juilliard, and so she lost her student housing. I offered to put her up for as long as she wanted at my place. But it was just a studio, and with Jeffy staying over half the time, it really wasn't a viable share. And that Biran came along with a magnificent full floor of a space—it was four times the size of my apartment, fourteen-foot ceilings, gigantic windows, and a baby grand piano in the corner. I have to assume that Biran had the piano brought in, just for Geffel. I don't think the place came with major appliances and a grand. It was a fabulous deal. Who wouldn't take it? You'd be silly not to—or wise to Biran's shenanigans, which Geffel kind of was, but wasn't totally.

She asked me what I thought she should do. I told her, "Listen, Geffel—it's a great space. Can I have it if you don't want it? Besides, it's just an apartment. There are a million more of them available in Manhattan. Grab it, and if it doesn't work out for any reason, you can get another place anywhere in the city the next day."

The way things eventually went down with Geffel and that Biran, I felt bad later for encouraging her to take the place. But, in my defense, it really was a beautiful space, and that seemed to outweigh the psychological ugliness of its sponsor. Geffel was tentative about taking it, wisely, but decided, also wisely, to seize the opportunity. It was bright and roomy—a big loft-style open space, with a separate area good for an office, and an excellent view of East 3rd Street, which was entertaining to watch in those days—a new drug deal to see every minute! The album cover [for Adrianne Geffel's eponymous debut release] gives you an idea of the layout. You know it?

[Athema is answered in the affirmative.]

The whole area in the photo above where you see Geffel at the piano, where her name was printed—that was all windows. And across the top, where it says, "Biran Zervakis Presents," there was an exquisite, detailed old pressed-tin ceiling—rusty, brownish-silvery unpainted tin. I loved to look up at it when I went to visit Geffel. It made me think of my own artwork at the time. It had never been painted, just like my canvases.

Harvé Mendelman
(Executive Vice President, Infini Records):

Didn't know Adry Geffel's music in great depth before her manager, Biran Zervakis, came to see me. Impressive individual. Very first time he came to the office, before he and I became good friends, he handled himself with class. Brought a bouquet of flowers for my secretary, Karen. That's *class*. Almost doesn't matter very much what the flowers cost—it's the gesture. It's a way of saying *Good afternoon, how do you do? Take note of me, if you will. I am an individual who appreciates goods things, and I am here to bring good things to you and your business, beginning with these flowers.*

Adry Geffel was an excellent fit in the roster of Infini Records artists that I would start to develop as an artist-and-repertoire executive after I signed her. You familiar with the history of the label? I understand you talked to my secretary now, Bethany, to schedule this interview. She told me you didn't say very much about what you think of our product. And you didn't even bring her flowers!

I'm just teasing with you. [Mendelman attempts to laugh.] It's by no means a prerequisite to come here with flowers! That's what makes it so meaningful when it's actually done.

In '78, '79, we were beginning to establish ourselves as a leading force in the field of contemporary music. You can read the whole history of the company in the in-depth advertorial all about us that I commissioned for *Billboard* magazine. I'll make sure you have a copy of it before you actually write about me.

[Mendelman calls through the door of his office to his assistant.] Bethany—Xerox a copy of the *Billboard* advertorial for the oral-history people, please. Thank you.

I believe it's important to say "Thank you," even to the people who work for you. It's a small thing, but to them, it means something, and it's cheaper than flowers! [Mendelman again attempts a laugh.]

When my good friend Biran Zervakis came to see me for the first time—we weren't friends at that stage . . . this is how it all began—and he told me about Adry Geffel, Infini was still just a hungry young label with a keen ear for fresh sounds. As a matter of fact, that's how I put it in *Billboard*. Only a few years before that, prior to my ascension in the ranks of the A&R Department, the company had been a relatively marginal but profitable label in the budget niche of the classical field. Specialized in the presentation of historical masterworks in the public domain, recorded by the many fine state-sponsored orchestras behind the Iron Curtain and made available to us through various channels. I was overseeing manufacturing and distribution, though I had attended a college with a strong music program and had the benefit of that association.

We here at Infini are deeply committed to the art of experimentation, on every level of production and presentation of our product. We not only facilitate experimentation by the artists in our catalog and promote the experimentation they do for us—as a record label, we ourselves are experiment*eurs*. We push the envelope. We *pull* the envelope. We tear it apart and smash it up into a little ball. You wouldn't know it even *was* an envelope. But *we* know.

At the time I was transitioning out of manufacturing into A&R, I took notice of the fact that we had accumulated a number of tapes with technical *idiosyncrasies*. Had a recording from Czechoslovakia of Schubert, if you've heard of him, recorded at a warbling speed, a session of the Hungarian State Philharmonic playing something that couldn't be properly identified because a system overload had produced a low, sustained buzz sound in place of the music. I looked over this material and challenged myself to apply myself creatively as an experimentative market-*eur*. I arranged for this material, along with a few other things with fascinating errors, to be packaged as the lead-off title in a new line we called *The Infini Archive of Anomalies of Musique Mechanique*. I commissioned liner notes from a professor at the New School for Social Research in Greenwich Village, who also gave us the name for the series. The records sold only modestly, but cost us very little, and you can't put a price tag on experimentation. That was the start of our *avant-line*, as I call it.

My friend Biran brought in several cassette recordings of performances by Adry Geffel at one of the lofts in SoHo. I thanked him and told him to leave them with me, and I would give them a listen, which is what I always told artists' reps, as a matter of policy, and, I'm proud to say, I sometimes did. Biran shook his head and put the tapes back in his briefcase. "No, no—never," he said.

Biran said, "These are priceless one-of-a-kind documents

of compositions impossible to duplicate. I would no longer leave them with a record-company executive, no matter how esteemed he may be, than I would leave them with the member of the audience who sneaked a recorder into the loft and made the tapes."

Now I was intrigued enough to want to hear the music. Called my secretary Karen in and had her play one of the cassettes on the stereo on my desk. I said, "Thank you, Karen"—*remember*—and leaned back in my chair to soak in the music.

Next minute, I was leaning in to hear the sound more closely. Minute later, I'm sitting straight up, shocked at the power of this music. It was like nothing I ever heard before. It was free. It was exciting. It was dissonant. It was painful. It was something different every minute. I told Karen to turn down the volume for a minute, to give me a break from it, and I said to Biran, "What is this, exactly? What music is she playing?"

Biran said, "She's playing what she's feeling. It isn't music as it has ever been known before. You could say it isn't music at all—it's pure feeling."

I instructed Karen to turn off the stereo, and I said to Biran, "Let's talk."

I said, "I'd like to see this person who makes this music that's not music. Let's make a plan to do that, and then we can all talk business."

Biran got a twinkle in his eye. I could tell there was something . . . *special* . . . on his mind when he talked about Adry Geffel. He called her "my Adry," and I think that says it all. Lowered his voice to a whisper, and said, "I'd love to surprise her with this. Let's work up the contract together, and we can bring it to her at her next concert, wrapped with a bow."

Karen Gigliardi
(former executive assistant, Infini Records):

Such a sweetheart, he was, that little Biran. Funny-looking, with that silly peanut of a chin he had, but who noticed? Such a *charmer*—you could see how a pretty girl like Adrianne could go for him, even if she might have done a lot better in the physical department.

He *doted* on her, took care of everything for her. All the business, the contracts, the paperwork, the decisions—*everything*. She didn't have to worry about a thing but her music and keeping him happy. He handed her everything on a big, polished, silver-plated platter—signed, sealed, and delivered.

Remember that song by Stevie Wonder? If he was on Infini Records, I would have died and gone to heaven! That's more my kind of music than the kind Mr. Mendelman got us into. He was what my late husband Doug used to call an *intellectual*. I would call Mr. Mendelman a lot of different things. Doug would call him "intellectual," and that was his prerogative. We didn't agree on a whole lot, Doug and me. I loved him even though we didn't have all that much in common, honestly—like Biran and Adrianne, you could say, though they were connected very closely forever by the record contracts. Doug and I were married, so we had our own contract, in a way—a marriage contract—but that's not as complicated as a record deal.

You could tell how much Adrianne meant to Biran. I didn't know they were living together at the beginning. All the original correspondence, in the beginning, he had me send to a lawyer's office. Then, he asked me to mail him things to his home address, which was on East 3rd Street. Tax time, I had to get a W-2 from Adrianne, and there it was, the *same address*. I should have known!

[Gigliardi is asked for her impressions of Adrianne Geffel and Biran Zervakis as a couple.]

Oh—I'd have to think . . . I'm not sure if I ever saw them together physically, in the same place. I can't really picture them together. Maybe once. Biran came to the office and took care of the business on his own, as long as she was on the label, and when she was dropped, I didn't see much of him for a while, till after Adrianne—how am I supposed to put this?—*went away*? He came around again after that, and he helped Mr. Mendelman with the albums they put together from all the . . . I guess the best word would be the dribs and drabs.

Biran Zervakis:

I know there's no need for me to tell you how wonderful Adry's records were and how gratifying it was for me to see my hard work for Adry reap the rewards it so dearly deserved. It's a matter of *record*, so to speak, that I produced all the albums released over the years under the contract I negotiated for us at Infini Records, from her debut release, named for Adry herself—we showcased her name in the actual title—and the others recorded live in the lofts and galleries to the beginning of her career in the studio, with *Chords and Baffling*, and on to the projects released more recently, comprising a variety of archival materials and outtakes I've edited on Adry's behalf.

I'll share with you how it all began. I could practically feel the creative energy of Adry's music bursting off the tape when I first found someone in the audience recording one of her loft concerts and brought the cassette home and played it. To set the record straight, incidentally, I did *not* push the woman on the floor to grab the tape from her. It would have been clear to anyone—if anyone had been looking, they could have seen that she lost her balance and fell. Yes, it's true, it might have been a very sweet gesture to pay her for the tape, but seriously, how much did a cassette tape cost in those days? A dollar ninety-nine?

[Zervakis is asked about the decision to use *Biran Zervakis Presents Adrianne Geffel* as the title of Geffel's first album.]

Thank you for pointing that out. I appreciated the fact that the album was titled that way, at the suggestion of one of the people involved in the production.

[Zervakis is asked if he was the person.)

I don't know who would deny that I was absolutely, most definitely involved in the production. That would be outrageous.

For the albums that followed that first one, I didn't want anyone to think I was trying to steal Adry's thunder, so I had that line removed, and we simply added a phrase below the title, "A Biran

Zervakis Presentation." As a matter of fact, the designer reduced the type size on that line for most of the records or one of them, I think. I didn't complain, not to Adry. I certainly didn't object to that in a public way. Adry—Adry . . . wonderful, pretty, capable in many ways—earned the credit I made sure she received as the primary creator of the albums. Someone knowledgeable would say, well, that goes without saying, but, don't forget, the producer is also a creator—to produce *is* to *make* something. But I'll leave that for others to say.

[Zervakis is asked about the publishing of Geffel's compositions.]

That's a woefully complicated question. I wouldn't want to tax your readers with such technical mumbo-jumbo. I can't tell you what it all means anyway. I shouldn't even try to tell you until all the suits are resolved. I can say this: Adry herself wrote the title for every one of her compositions. In that sense, she can be said to "hold title" to the music. She holds the titles! The underlying rights are surely another matter, legally. However, the titles themselves were totally her creation.

[Zervakis is reminded that copyright law does not protect titles.]

You're so right! As you know, apparently, it may not mean anything legally or financially to say that someone owns a title. But it means something to *me* to be able to say to you here today that, however complicated the rights to Adry's music may be, it was my Adry alone who came up with the titles.

Harvé Mendelman:

See for yourself—the packaging was first-class, four-color, on every title in the entire Adrianne Geffel catalog here at Infini. Even the one with the plain white cover and lettering, we had printed on a color-capable press, during the press downtime. That's the kind of class we put into our product.

[Mendelman gestures toward a row of five Geffel album jackets framed and hanging on a wall.]

The photography—*artistic*. The typography, the printing, the card stock, the lamination, everything—*artistic*. Look at *So Far, SoHo*, the second one, right there.

[Mendelman points to the wall.]

That's the cover we commissioned from Ann Athema. We printed her description of what the art would look like in a box of text in the right corner. If you get close to it, you can read it. It's not very long. In most of the stores, it ended up covered by the price sticker, so the album cover looked blank, but that never hurt sales from people who mistook it for the Beatles' "White Album." And next to it—see [the album titled] *Oh, Negative*—the way the title is painted in red? That's actually blood that Athema's artist friend Marina Abramovic used like finger paint to make the lettering. We had it photographed and superimposed above Adrianne's head in the cover photo. The original idea was to hand-paint the title on every copy of the album in the blood, but—I don't want to sound harsh, but we were hoping to sell more copies than you could paint with the blood you'd get from a single artist.

Every package—*artistic.* And inside—pure *Adrianne Geffel.* Before every one of her albums was released into the marketplace, I listened to it all the way to the end. Forgive me for boasting, but that's the truth, and it wasn't easy, let me tell you. Have you heard her music—I mean, actually listened to it without other, normal music playing at the same time, to drown it out? It's no fun to do. But I've done it myself, for every album. Not straight through in one sitting—I took breaks and came back when I was ready to take some more. And I have to say that, even though I can't claim to understand what she was playing or *like* it, quote unquote, I appreciate the music for its uniqueness and its value to the culture and our record company—and I'm talking not only in terms of branding and revenue, but also market share.

Ann Athema:

Geffel the recording artist—now one of us was officially an artist. I knew a fair number of *art-making* artists from Cooper Union and the galleries and the bars, but Geffel was the first person I knew who became a *recording* artist. It was as if being known for making recordings *made* her an artist in the eyes of the world, and not merely a person playing music of a kind the world had never known before, in somebody's loft. It elevated Geffel's visibility so dramatically that I was almost thankful to that Biran for setting up the deal. But I wasn't.

You've heard the records, so you know the first couple of them were pressed from tape recordings someone in the audience made.

There was a story in the *SoHo News* that Biran wrote a big check to the person who made the tapes, to acquire the rights. Jon Geldman wrote that up. I saw Geldman at one of Geffel's shows and he said, "It's true—Biran told me so himself." So . . .

Geffel asked me if I would do the artwork for her second album, and I loved the idea. It made no sense. She gave me the title, *So Far, SoHo*, and I wrote up a little description of what the art would be, so the record company could print it on the cover. I wrote: "Abstractions, egos, and dreams, eight square blocks wide, four feet deep, and half a million people high." I read it to Geffel, and she said, "Exquisite! Now, tell Biran he can have it for five hundred dollars," and I did. I never got the check, and I told Jon Geldman, but *that*, he didn't write up.

When Geffel went in to record her first studio album, she invited me to watch, and I went. The studio was on the fourth or fifth floor of an old industrial building on Broadway, off Prince Street. There was a wholesale electronics distributor on the ground floor. I know that's not particularly helpful information, since there were wholesale distributors on the street level of every building in SoHo. We got to the studio a little late, because I wanted to make sure Geffel had something in her stomach before the recording session, and we couldn't find a restaurant or coffee shop anywhere. There was no place to eat in SoHo, unless you had an appetite for wholesale supplies. We still had to wait for quite a while in the studio, because Biran had not yet arrived.

They were both living in the 3rd Street apartment at this point. He told her he had some sort of trouble with his family at home, and he needed a place to crash, and asked Geffel if he could stay in her little office room temporarily, and she felt like she couldn't say no, since he got her the place. You'd think they would show up at the studio together, since they were coming from the same place. But I'm sure Geffel left on her own, while he was getting his beauty sleep.

Geffel was wearing one of the headscarves she usually wore on the street, to keep out ambient music. She unraveled it with a swirl of a dancerly flourish and announced, "I'm ready—where's the piano?" The engineer told us he had strict orders from the producer, Mr. Zervakis, to do nothing without him. We just sat there for almost an hour, sweating on the plastic sofa, waiting for that Biran to show up. Geffel was getting agitated and started bobbing her head back and forth and patting her hands on her legs to the beat of whatever music she was hearing in her head. By the time Biran walked in, she was humming something loud and strange.

Biran gave us a big, ridiculous grin, waltzed into the control room, and started gabbing with the engineer. After another ten or fifteen minutes, he came out and said, "Hope you ladies are hungry—I just had some Chinese ordered in for us. It should be here in half an hour."

Geffel rose up slowly, put her face in front of Biran, and said, "If we're not recording in half a *minute*, I'm gone."

The engineer brought Geffel into the recording studio, and Biran followed them in. And the engineer moved into the control room and started pushing buttons and moving levers. Biran stayed with Geffel, and I watched them from the control room through the giant glass window. Geffel settled in on the piano bench and tested out the keyboard while Biran walked around the space, examining random things like a night student in an improv class doing a hammy Sherlock Holmes skit. He tapped the microphone positioned over the piano. He bounced his hands along the baffling on the walls and squeezed a pair of the foam pyramids like they were little boobs. He blew his breath onto the glass window to the control room and, when some condensation formed, drew a smiley face with two buck teeth on the smile. Tapping onto the window, he yelled to the engineer, "Roll tape!" He leaned back against the glass nonchalantly and waved a finger at Geffel. She gave him an icy glare and, with her eyes still locked on him, started to play.

You know from the album how fiery Geffel was at that moment. She improvised the whole piece that takes up half the first side of the record in one take. A couple of times, I almost burst in to stop things, for Geffel's sake. She was hurling fire straight at Biran, and he just smiled, leaning on the glass with his hands in his pockets like he was watching the sunset on his veranda, and that only made her rage even more. I got up close to the window glass, so Geffel could see me, and shrugged my shoulders to send a message of "Who cares? Don't let him bother you." That seemed to calm her down. Then Biran turned around to the window and blew his breath on the glass again, and drew a heart with an arrow going through it, and turned back to Geffel and grinned. She sounded like she could break the piano. That's the track they titled "Pane Relief."

N. D. Nieve (former music critic, the *Village Voice*):

There's a kinetic audacity of a rarefied kind in Adrianne Geffel's music—an unpredictability, an indeterminacy, an instability, and an uncertainty that, when you listen close, are truly neither "un" nor "in." Her records are a free assault on everything that recording itself represents. They're not formal statements, inscribed for the ages in musical notation for entombment in the great canon of canonicality. They're screams, and they're whispers. They're outbursts so vital, so mind-rattling, soul-fuckingly extreme that they burst out and fly straight through you and out of your room and around the whole world with so much speed and power that they come back into your house from the other direction, and never knock. They're more than outbursts—they're inside-outbursts, outsider-artbursts. They're artsider out . . . *art* . . . All that.

Adrianne Geffel's music is . . . Adrianne Geffel's music is music with *no fear*. Music with no inhibitions—no category, no name, no shape, no disguises, no adornments, no clothes. It's naked—a nudie show for the brain. It's in your face—and up your ass all the way up into your face, going from the inside.

What do I think of Adrianne Geffel's music? What *can* I think? How could I begin to answer that?

[Nieve is reminded that he first began to write about Geffel's music in 1980 and that he appears to be at no loss for words presently.]

That's right, and I think I've said it all.

Dr. Stewart A. Rauschmittel, Ph.D. (visiting lecturer, New School for Social Research):

I have been studying the music of Adrianne Geffel for many years. Indeed, my interest in the strategies manifest in her work precedes the so-called "making" of the work itself. I have examined the broad spectrum of modality narratives negotiated and renegotiated by the music associated with Adrianne Geffel. I refer you to my monograph, *Spinning Discourses: Toward a Theory of the Rubric of Disequilibrium in Avant-Garde Text and Pretext*, published by the University of California, Santa Cruz. I recommend to you, also, the essay I was commissioned to write as liner notes for the series of recordings issued under my oversight as *The Infini Archive of Anomalies of Musique Mechanique*. It will give you some understanding of my approach to a set of issues unrelated to Adrianne Geffel and the work connected with her.

The sheer volume of scholarship on Adrianne Geffel since recordings made her music available for close examination speaks at once to the emotional-intellectual capaciousness of the work and to the inversely proportionate illuminative capacity of the musicologists engaged in unpacking it. To unpack work of such a nature properly, I contend, one needs first to grasp it, then unlock it, and open it up. Only at that point can it be unpacked. More challenging, still, is the task of repacking when it's time to go home, and now everything won't fit back in.

In my view, Adrianne Geffel may best be thought of as the

living embodiment of aesthetic disjunction iterated across cognitive and spatial-economic planes. Perhaps I should qualify that. Is she still living?

[Rauschmittel is told Geffel's status is unknown at the time of this interview.]

I see. In either event, Adrianne Geffel brings to mind Adorno's *Philosophie der neuen Musik*, in which he characterized avant-garde music as constituting what, in German, is referred to as *Flaschenpost*.

[Rauschmittel is asked what that means.]

As I've pointed out, it's a German term. I would need to look that up.

If you're curious to know more about my thinking on Adrianne Geffel, you are free to read my writings on the subject. It's all written in English, so you won't have to ask what any of the words mean. I've written about Geffel and her music in a number of journals, including the *Journal of American Musicology*, *Musicological America*, the *Journal of Musicological Studies*, and *Studies in Musicology*. I did also write an essay of liner notes for the first album of Adrianne Geffel's music released by Infini Records, at the request of the label's director, Harvé Mendelman. However, my essay was not used. In its place, there was a work of writing of a certain character by the producer of the recording, Biran Zervakis, in which he expounded with prolixity on his role in facilitating Geffel's career in performance and recordings. I don't feel qualified to comment on that as a musicologist. I suggest you find a psychiatrist.

Thomas Mann, responding to Adorno, wrote of what he saw as a pattern of elliptical self-destruction and self-perpetuation in the cultural economy of the musical vanguard. He called the avant-garde "the vanguard of the army it attacks." I'm hoping someday to develop an analytical framework to connect that to Adrianne Geffel. As of yet, the connection escapes me.

Carolyn Geffel:

As a mother, I would have to say it stung a bit to go so long without hearing from Adry. She could have written us at any time—she had our mailing address. It used to be *her* address, too! It still *was* her address, as far as her father and I were concerned. Our home would always be our daughter's home, and speaking as the person responsible for the bookkeeping in our household, that's what I told the IRS when we claimed Adry as a dependent in those years. So, as a mother, yes, I missed her. Even her father missed her, you could say. I picked that up sometimes.

As a businesswoman, I could understand that Adry had to have a lot of serious responsibilities taking up her time as a professional entertainer. Just look at how much I have on my plate every day to take care of all the paperwork for our propane business—and the merchandising *and* the taxes and everything else Greg says he's too busy to do, with whatever *he's* doing with *his* time when I'm not looking, though it's just as well, because I'm very good at what I do. Adry obviously inherited that from me. She's *all* me! I'm so proud of her!

Greg and I talked about making a trip back to New York to see one of Adry's performances in that area where she was performing, if the public was allowed. We weren't clear on all that. Nina Oberheimer came over to the house one day and showed us an article in a music magazine about Adry, and I used the Xerox machine to copy it, and framed it in our office. Just around the same time, Nina brought us a record album Adry made and we were so proud, we framed that, too. They're both still hanging in the same place, right under the plaques we won when we were named as a Finalist and Second Finalist for Fuel Dealership of the Year in the Western Pennsylvania district. That was for two separate years—I can show you before you leave.

[Geffel is asked to share her thoughts on the music on the album.]

That's such a smart question! I can see *you're* good at what *you* do, too! I'd have to take it off the wall and unframe it, and get the record player out, to be able to listen to it. But it could be worth the trouble!

Nina Oberheimer:

What's the phrase—"the student surpassed the teacher"? That's the way I'd like to think of the music of Adrianne's I heard on the records I bought when I read about her career in New York. I'd like to think that way, but I'm not sure I can. I played the records, and I didn't quite feel like Adrianne had surpassed me. I felt like she had taken another road and went in a completely different direction than the music I studied and devoted my life to teaching. Nothing in my musical education at Clarion prepared me for the sound of those records. Adrianne and I were in two different places much further from each other than Venango County and New York City.

Jon Geldman:

By the time of her third or fourth album—by *Oh, Negative*, certainly—Adrianne Geffel was so firmly established as a phenomenon of the music world in New York that people nearly forgot the importance of my role in introducing her, until I reminded them. It became exhausting. I reviewed all the records she made, and covered literally every one of her concerts that I could get press comps for. Pulling together all that writing for the book I'm compiling, I was struck by how frequently and how perceptively I've written about Geffel's music.

The competition heated up for me. Since her music was so unique and stood outside the standard categories, writers on every music beat felt free to grab a piece of her, and they all acted like they discovered her. The arrogance was appalling. I remember going to the press event Infini Records set up at the K. Lewitt Gallery for the anniversary of her debut there. You weren't there, I know. I suppose you were still in school then, though this was in July, so you might have been in summer camp.

[Geldman is prompted to continue with his recollection.]

All the New York press was there. The classical-music writers were all there from *Time* magazine and *Saturday Review*, trying to figure out what to make of this woman—good Lord, man, a *woman*!—playing such volatile music. The rock critics were there from *Rolling Stone* and the other rags, mumbling about how the fury and brutal force of her music proved she was a punk rocker in disguise. Cultural critics were on the hunt for political subtext and social implications in her music. Susan Sontag was there, huddled in a corner with Twyla Tharp, but left before Adrianne played, when Leon Wieseltier came in and Tharp glommed onto him. So many people came that there was a mob of about ten or twelve people standing outside the gallery, waiting to get in. The sight of all those people on the streets of SoHo was disorienting.

Adrianne Geffel seemed pretty shaken up herself, in the center of all the hubbub. I worked my way through the crowd to talk to her. I never even got to her. She was pacing around—dancing really, practically—until she was introduced to play. When she did, she just simply exploded at the piano. In my piece on the event, I wrote that she "imploded," to put a twist on the word. I've expanded the piece for inclusion in my anthology, adding some of my impressions of the various critics and others who were there.

Ruth Sirotta LeMat:

The office of the Music Department at the School of the Arts at NYU, where I taught, carried subscriptions to a number of scholarly periodicals, and we in the faculty were permitted to take the older editions for our private use when the new editions arrived. On occasion, I would bring a copy of the *Journal of American Musicology* home with me. It was turgid but printed on high-quality paper. When my brother's daughter Stephanie visited, I liked to use the articles for origami. I was cutting out pages one morning, in anticipation of Stephanie's arrival, and I found a critical study of a recording by Adrianne in the journal. This was the first I learned of Adrianne's recording career. I was greatly heartened to read of this, and went out the next day to purchase a copy of the album. If you'd care to read the article, I saved it. If you'd like it, I can flatten it out in a book overnight and give it to you.

I thought the album was fresh and original. The music was forceful and, as always for Adrianne but more so than I had ever heard before, profoundly emotive and difficult to process. I found the music to be almost unbearably emotional and challenging. I couldn't have been more pleased for Adrianne. Listening to that record also led me to wonder how she was doing, generally speaking. The emotionality of the music was very deep and somewhat dark.

I hadn't had a mailing address for Adrianne since she withdrew from Juilliard. Uncertain how to reach her, I wrote a letter to her and mailed it to her attention, care of the record company. I never received a response. After a month or so, I wrote a second letter and again mailed it to the record company. I did this several times over a period of more than a year, and received nothing in response. I worried that the letters might not have been getting to Adrianne.

I learned the truth and was far from happy about it when I

finally saw her again. There was a new venue for music in the Lincoln Center vicinity called Merkin Hall. It's still there today and remains the same willfully *outré* hostel for adventurism in the New York concert world. When the hall first opened, one of my composition students was doing volunteer work in the box office, because it attracted a conservatory audience and was thought of as a hot classical-music pickup spot. This student saw that Adrianne was scheduled to be giving a concert, and told me about it. To the best of my knowledge, it was Adrianne's first performance in a major concert hall, if not her first performance north of Houston Street.

My student had the rehearsal schedule and let me in early on the day of Adrianne's rehearsal. I was waiting in the lobby for her when a peculiar young man came in and announced himself as Adrianne's manager and instructed everyone but the technical crew to vacate. I started to head out the door when Adrianne entered. She saw me and simply froze for a moment. I reached my arms out and gave her a big, tight hug, and she nestled her head on my shoulder. She said to me, "Oh, Mrs. LeMat . . ." Her voice was quaking. She said, "Thank you so much for your letters. I'm sorry for not answering you. I just didn't know what to say. I don't know what to *think* anymore. I'm sorry . . ."

Harvé Mendelman:

The PR show we did at the Lewitt Gallery got us sensational press. *Time* magazine called her the "new Queen of Bleak Chic."

When you say it like I am to you now, it sounds good. You have to know how to pronounce "chic," like you're French. If you say it in English—"Bleak Chick"—it's not as clever. That's not so bad, either, though. Of all the chicks around the music scene, Adry Geffel was the bleakest.

We at Infini Records recognized this as the opportune time to take Adry Geffel up to the next level and present her in a major venue for a major concert album. Nothing against the lofts and galleries—I liked Milijenko Jervic, and I wasn't even that much into coke at that time. But a loft does not a concert hall make, and vice versa. My good friend Biran and I put our heads together, and we produced the big concert at Merkin Hall. You would know it as "The Merkin Concert," which is the title we used on the album. One of the salesmen, a real wisenheimer, told me we should call it "Adry's Merkin," assuming I didn't know that "merkin" meant something besides the name of the guy who paid for the hall. When Karen explained it to me, I told him to cut out the funny business and stick to the money business.

We gave the concert a major advertising push, far outspending the promotional allocation reserved in Adry's advance budget. It was an investment in her career much more meaningful to those of us responsible for her marketing than mere cash in her pocket. A writer for the *Daily News* did an article with a nice plug for the concert, and that got picked up by the AP and syndicated around the country. People were phoning in for tickets long-distance, just to see Adrianne Geffel.

Biran Zervakis:

Those were the days of all-enveloping togetherness for my magical Adry and me. We were living together in the home I found for us in Greenwich Village. The writers were all so curious about our relationship—"Tell us, please, would you, are the two of you living as husband and wife?" I'd say, "Now, now—why even try to put a label on any relationship?" I'd say, "But if you must, you can think of Adry and I as living as *man* and *woman*." Our relationship could only be described as something—some . . . *thing*—that was the relationship between us.

Adry put it all in her music. Just listen to the "Merkin Concert" album we made from the first half of the performance.

Ruth Sirotta LeMat:

I was distraught to have to miss the concert. By the time I learned about it from my student, it was already sold out. I was hoping to be able to hear the rehearsal, but I got booted out by Adrianne's manager.

Ann Athema:

Geffel gave the record company my name for a comp ticket, so I was able to get in. It actually wasn't a comp, though, I found out at tax time, when I got a 1099 from Infini Records for fifteen dollars of income. I called Mendelman, and he explained to me the cost of the ticket had been logged as my payment for the art he had commissioned from me for Geffel's album, *So Far, SoHo*. I said, "I see. Thank you. Well . . . when you're ready to package your next release, I have a new artwork that I've created specifically with Infini in mind." I said, "It's a portrait of your soul—half human, one-quarter rabid dog, and one-quarter pure emptiness—burning in hell while Satan twists his pitchfork into your ass."

The concert was packed. There was electricity in the air, and lots of new faces I didn't recognize from the shows in SoHo. My seat was close to the back—*thanks again*, Mendelman—but that had its benefits, because I could watch the audience, along with Geffel, and it was fascinating to see how people reacted to the unusual music she made. The lights went down, and the room fell quiet. Out from the wings came that Biran, and he started yammering about how *grateful* he was to everyone who came tonight and how *gratifying* it was for him to work so *intimately* with Adrianne Geffel since he first recognized her genius *before anyone else* understood her . . . I was about to puke. He was still talking when Geffel came out from the other side of the stage. She walked right past him, sat down at the piano, and started playing. She already launched a violent assault on the keyboard before he got to announce her name. He turned in her direction and applauded, but she kept her eyes on the keyboard, and everyone else kept quiet, so they could hear her.

I've never quite understood Geffel's music—you know that. It doesn't exactly fall easily on the ears. This show was especially odd and severe. I knew Geffel well enough to know she was clearly not in a good place emotionally. She played straight through for nearly half an hour—all the music on the live album. She paused for a moment to catch her breath, and someone in the audience yelled out, "Play 'Models and Muggers'!"

Geffel took her hands off the keyboard and turned to the audience. She looked all around, squinting and trying to find the person who said that.

About ten rows ahead of me, a young woman raised her hand. She said, softly, "I'm right here, Adry."

Geffel rose up from the piano and announced to the audience, "Thank you, everyone. We'll have a fifteen-minute intermission, and I'll be back to play more music."

The woman who had called out to her stood up. She and Adry locked eyes, and Adry burst into a smile I had never ever seen before.

CHAPTER 7

Sweet Smells

(1982–1984)

Barbara Lucher:

Have you heard the second part of that concert?

[Lucher is answered in the negative.]

I know you never heard it, because you weren't there. If you weren't fucking *there*, you couldn't fucking *hear it*, because the fucking *record company* didn't put it on the fucking *record*. And you know why?

(Lucher is prompted to answer the question herself.]

Oh, God . . . I hate you. Do you want to hear about this or not?

[Lucher is answered in the affirmative.]

Then shut the fuck up and let me talk. The record company didn't release the second part of the concert because it didn't meet their approval, and that was because they're assholes. That's the story. Next question.

[Lucher is asked to recount the circumstances that led her to attend the Adrianne Geffel concert at Merkin Hall.]

I bought a ticket over the phone. It was open to the public, wasn't it? *Don't answer that*, if you're just going to ask me another goddamn question.

Try to follow me. Okay—I was basically pissed off at the world. I was pissed at myself for missing that other concert at Juilliard that we talked about. I was pissed at my shit-for-brains father—shit for brains and shittier shit for balls, that guy—for the way he took my car away from me. I was pissed at my own self for not using my own brains, which are *not* made of shit, if you don't know, and I should have figured out a way to get to New York anyway. I knew Adry would be hurt and mad at me for not being there, and I was mad about that. I was mad in a whole lot of ways, and the more I thought about it all, the madder I got.

But I missed her. You know . . . I missed her. So I wrote her a letter, to the address of the building I moved her into when she started at Juilliard, and the letter came back as undeliverable. So I wrote her again, care of the school, but I never heard back. Eventually, after Adry and I reconnected and talked about things, we put two and two together and realized they added up to the name Zervakis. We figured he must've been intercepting the letters and keeping them from her. But I didn't know that when it was happening. I was writing to her and not hearing back, that's what I knew. Adry said she wrote to me, too, and Zervakis was taking her mail and telling her he was bringing it to the post office and chucking it or rolling cigars with it and smoking it or whatever the fuck he did for the sicko pleasure he got from taking advantage of Adry.

After a while, I presumed she must have gotten all caught up in her new life in New York and forgot about me. It was a hard time, but I kept myself occupied. I got a new job—an actual job, after [having been employed at] Denny's, working for some builders in the county called Kev-Rew Construction. It was named for the owners, Kevin and Andrew. I called both the guys "Kev-Rew," to annoy them, and they would just stare at me, because they didn't know what to make of a girl like me, and I learned a lot about carpentry from them. I was doing pretty nicely, got my own car, a used '79 Chevy Chevette, in green and rust—not rust the color, rust the condition of the shitty Chevy tin-foil body. There was an article about Adry from one of the New York papers picked up in the *Harrisburg Patriot-News*. My mom showed it to me. I read that and saw about the concert coming up in the city, and I said to myself, *Well, fuckety-fuck . . . I'm going.*

Biran Zervakis:

As my attorneys have spelled out in their correspondence to you, which I presume you have shared with your own attorneys—you do have attorneys, I presume . . . If you don't, I highly recommend you retain one before you attempt to have your book published, if you're at all serious about quoting me. No author or writer with any credibility could ever write about my Adry without quoting me. That goes without saying. In other words, there's no need for me to even say it. Accordingly, as I've explained, I hope you've retained a lawyer, if you're financially equipped to do that. If you're not, I understand. An oral historian must make very little money.

To recap, as my attorneys have laid out plainly, there are certain subjects I have been advised against discussing for publication. Barbara Lucher is foremost among them. I can safely say this: Barbara Lucher stole my Adry from me. I mean that not in any business sense. Matters of that nature, I can't and shan't discuss.

[Zervakis is prompted to elaborate on the matters not pertaining to business.]

She literally stole her, just as literally as anyone has ever stolen anything that ever belonged to anyone else. Let's leave it at that. There's no need to say any more. The woman drove me out of my own home! The very first time I ever met her, which by mercy should have been the last, I came home to the apartment my Adry and I both called home—the property on East 3rd Street made famous internationally from the exquisite depiction of it on the cover of the first album I produced for Adry—and the two of them were already there, in our home, alone.

[Zervakis is asked if he is referring to the night of the Merkin Hall concert.]

Yes, of course. There's no need to rub it in. I entered the apartment, exactly as I always did every time I walked in, and Adry and that woman were sitting at the kitchen table drinking wine and talking. Adry must have known I was weary from the stress of the evening. She suggested I get some rest in my room. Lucher, without so much as a proper greeting, chimed in, "Listen to the girl now. Go to your room!"

I was exhausted and decided on my own accord—take note, *decided on my own accord*—to retire alone. I closed the door to my room and went to bed, but I was barely able to get a moment's rest all night. I could hear the two of them at the kitchen table, talking and laughing, talking and laughing . . . After hours on end of this, they finally stopped, and I heard the door to Adry's room close. I went out to get a drink of water and couldn't help but notice that Lucher's handbag was still on the table, with her wallet and an oval-shaped hairbrush and a few odds and ends in it, and I heard a variety of sounds coming from Adry's room. For the sake of discretion, I won't go into detail. You'll have to imagine for yourself what it's like to hear two young women having sex for hours. I couldn't sleep with that going on, not even after I went back to bed.

In the morning, when I came out of my room, the two of them were back at the kitchen table, talking and laughing again. It was revolting. Adry introduced us, but made an odd slip and referred to me as "Brian." Lucher looked over at me and said, "Brian—what will you be making us for breakfast?" I was *furious*. The audacity of calling me "Brian"! Did she think she was my *mother*? My mother never had sex with Adry. I stormed out the door and didn't come back till late that night. Adry moved out of the apartment that day, while I was gone, but I'm under advisement not to discuss that.

Ann Athema:

You remember, I first met Geffel at the Neurological Institute? We were the closest of friends from that point on. I still think of her as my closest friend—even now, when I can't call her or go for walks around the Lower East Side with her. Geffel is still the sublimest, to me. Even so, I feel like I didn't quite know her until I saw her with Barb Lucher. I think Geffel was truly at her happiest when she was with Barb. She was always sublime. But sublimity and happiness aren't the same.

I didn't realize who Barb was when I first saw her, yelling out from her seat at Merkin Hall, and I didn't know how important she was to Geffel until the day after, when Geffel called me. She even sounded different on the phone. She was talking, but almost singing. She said she wanted me to meet her and Barb at Dimicci's. It was early in the day, and Jeffy was over. Geffel said to bring him along, and we all squeezed around one of the tiny round tables the size of a dinner plate at Dimicci's. I got biscotti. Barb picked it up off my napkin, turned it all around and examined it, and said, "Does this look like a dick? I can't tell—I haven't seen a lot of dicks." Adry started laughing that funny laugh of hers, and we all cracked up, and Adry picked up the biscotti and put it in Barb's mouth.

We stayed at Dimicci's for hours, talking and drinking espresso and cappuccino and fellating biscotti. By the time we left, we had hatched a plan together for Adry to move out of the apartment on 3rd Street. We had it all figured out. It was like playing a party game with New York real estate, which, I've heard, some people uptown do for a living. We all went to 3rd Street and packed Adry up, and she and Barb went to my place on Ludlow Street to stay for a while. I went with Jeffy to his apartment on Ninth Avenue. This was temporary, to give Barb time to move her things in from Pennsylvania. At the end of the month, which was two or three weeks away, Adry and Barb would take over Jeffy's place, and Jeffy would move in with me. It didn't quite sink in to any of us that we had just made a set of major decisions about our relationship statuses—or stati, if that's a word. I hope it's not.

Jeffrey Knudsen:

Adry and Barb took over my apartment, and I moved in with Ann. I was happy to get out of there. It was on 17th and Ninth, a little bit north of the Meatpacking District. My uncle got it for me. He was connected to the butcher's union. The apartment belonged to a guy who was part of the union, and he died or something, and my uncle set me up with the place. It was not what you'd call a luxury apartment. It was more what you'd call a dump, but it was rent-controlled, and it was cheap. I just had to pay the rent by money order, because the lease was in the dead guy's name. I had to sign his name. His name was Carmine Trembler, and I had to sign his name the way he'd sign it, which I just guessed. I practiced up a signature, so the handwriting didn't look like mine. I can still do the signature, actually, if you want to see.

It smelled like meat all day and night. As dumps go, this one was disgusting.

The businesses around there were things like auto-body shops and different industry-supply stores, plate-glass companies, and a liquor store on every block for the workers at break time. There was an elevated railroad that was originally for moving cargo that would come from the piers directly into the factories and businesses that were around there. The elevated track was still standing, but it hadn't been used in years. It was totally abandoned—rusty, all beat up. So at night there were a lot of hookers working in the shadows under the elevated tracks, and horny men from the [Holland and Lincoln] tunnels driving over to avail themselves of the hookers. It was a totally industrial area—car parts sales and service and that kind of thing in the daytime, and the sex business at night. There wasn't a person with an artistic temperament in sight, other than the drag queens turning tricks.

It wasn't a great area, but Adry and Barb were fine with it. Barb was a really good carpenter and damn near gutted the place and rebuilt it. Ann and I went back a couple of months after Barb got her hands on it, and we couldn't believe it was the same place. She built a loft bed and a closet, and in the main room, by the kitchen area, she made an island for cooking. It was really nice and homey. You were in there, and the meat smell from outside was suddenly alright—it felt like somebody was making dinner.

Ray Octavio
(superintendent, 112–126 Ninth Avenue, retired):

Thank you for the opportunity to talk to me. My wife said you wrote a very nice letter. She remembers the ladies in the letter. I also remember these ladies. The short-haired one of them, I know better. There was nothing wrong with her—nothing wrong with both these ladies. I can vouch for them. The short-haired one did some work for me in the building sometimes. She was a good lady carpenter.

I was the super for those buildings for thirty-two years. Now I am disabled. This is legal by the State of New York. My wife did all the papers just like they make you do it.

[Octavio is prompted to describe his interactions with Geffel and Lucher.]

When they moved in, I don't remember. What I saw was the short-haired lady carrying big piles of lumber into the building. I had to know what she was doing. It was my responsibility. She told me she was making a fancy bed in her apartment, and she showed me the plans—professional plans, like a professional job, she did by herself. I could tell from my experience in this work that the lady knew what she was doing. I let her do her work. I didn't bother her. I looked at the job when it was over, and it was very professional. I told her, "Do you want to do some work in this building?" and she said, "Yes, Mr. Octavio, I would very much like to work for you," and I gave her jobs to do and gave her a little something from the money I was paid.

Barb Lucher:

Jeffy's place was a shithole in a big shitty shit-ass of an area. But man, fuck, it was a bargain. All we had to do was pretend to be Jeffy pretending to be some man named Carmine Trembler, and sign his name once a month, and we were sitting pretty fuckin' pretty. I have to tell you, we were sitting in a truly pretty place when I got done with it. I built a loft bed, so there would be room underneath to put a piano for Adry. I got the idea from the abandoned elevated railroad outside, and copied the design of that. The railroad structure was just going to waste, so I put it to use as my design. Somebody may as well use it for *something*. Then I called a piano mover and had the piano in the 3rd Street apartment trucked across town, and I had the bill sent to Zervakis. He flipped his little hair-gelled wig. I told him to deduct the cost from the money he still owed me for my share of the payout from Sony for their stealing the idea of the Walkman from me.

We made a beautiful little life. Neither one of us could cook a damn thing, but we figured out enough to get by and sometimes actually by accident made something good. I liked to chop stuff—it's almost like hammering—so I did that, and Adry fried it up. Adry—no surprise—liked to experiment with weird combinations of ingredients. There was a grimy old bodega a block and a half from us, the closest thing to a grocery store in the area. They carried shit like Pop Tarts, canned red beans, pineapple soda, and plantain chips, all with expiration dates in the 1970s. That was their whole stock in its entirety. One time, Adry got the inspiration to make a dinner out of that—Pop Tarts with red beans, garnished with plantain chips and served with a can of pineapple soda. She was better at music.

Adry, you know, was a big reader. I told you that, from high school. We liked to walk around the Village, and we saw a crowd of women gathered in front of a bookstore on Waverly Place. A writer died, and someone was standing on the sidewalk reading from one of her books. [Editor's note: Feminist author Djuna Barnes died in Greenwich Village on June 18, 1983. On the first anniversary of her death, a reading in her honor was held at the bookstore Three Lives and Company, which had previously gone by the name Djuna Books, in tribute to Barnes.]

Adry went back to the store a lot after that and loved it there. I'd drop her off, go run some errands, and come back hours later, and she'd be sitting there, reading and humming a happy tune or wrapped up in conversation with one of the women there. It was a big lesbian hangout. But so was the hardware store where I got supplies, Garber Hardware. Half the fucking Village was a lesbian hangout. The other half was for the gay boys. It was very different from the area where we actually lived, on 17th Street—nobody was there, straight or gay or undetermined. But we liked it, because it was quiet, and it was all ours.

We were happy together. I got pretty busy with carpentry work. I had business cards printed up with my own logo, Barb the Builder, and Adry dove into her music with a whole new kind of enthusiasm. The apartment was a big-ass project for me. I could handle the carpentry, but I wasn't a plumber, and the toilet had a hairline crack and seeped toilet water onto the floor every time you flushed. Good thing Adry knew a guy in music who did plumbing, Philip Glass. He came over and replaced the toilet for us, and when he saw the carpentry I had done in the place, he was so impressed he hooked me up with a New York contractor he used to work for, and they gave me a lot of work. I heard that he got a kickback for the referral, but that's totally legit, and I don't want to disparage Philip Glass for that. He was a good guy and a damn good plumber.

I needed a place to do my carpentry, where I wouldn't get sawdust all over the apartment. I got the super, Ray, to give me a key to the roof, so I could work up there. I set up a workshop on the roof. I'd work up there while Adry played piano or read books at home.

One night in the summer, the first year we were there, Adry and I were in the apartment, and I said, "Come with me—I want to show you something." I brought her up the service stairway to the roof and unlocked the door. During the day, I had framed out a platform bed with some lumber, and snuck up some bedding and pillows. Adry plopped right down on the bed, and said, "It's nice to know a gal who's good with tools."

I locked the service door behind us, and Adry and I laid there together on our backs. We looked up at the sky and saw a couple of stars poking through the mucky New York haze, and listened to the sounds of the West Side Highway traffic in the distance.

The sun came up, and I was awoken by the sound of a morning bird chirping a happy tune. I looked around to see where the bird was, and I realized it was Adry. Fast asleep, she was making the prettiest sounds I've ever heard.

Jon Geldman:

You can read all about that strange period in Adrianne Geffel's career in my book, *Geldman on Geffel*, when it's published. [Editor's note: In correspondence following this interview, Geldman requested that any reference to the prospective title *Geldman on Geffel* be accompanied by a clarification that Geldman's book in progress might be published under the title *Geffel by Geldman*.] The book will include my review of the Merkin Hall concert, which was not published in the *SoHo News* when I wrote it. The book will be the first time the review will be available to the reading public. It should be a big selling point for the book.

The decision not to print the review at the time of the concert was certainly not mine. It was the editor's call, and I thought it was misguided. She wanted me to add text to the review, even though I had written it to the assigned word count of eight hundred words. She asked me to cut part of what I written and add a whole new paragraph describing the second half of the show. I had no intention of doing that, because I considered myself committed to Adrianne Geffel and had no interest in publishing something negative about her. I only wrote negatively about her when I absolutely had to—I had no choice, in the shows after Merkin. It pained me dearly to be the one to criticize Geffel so strongly, but it had to be done, and I knew other critics would be doing it. I didn't want to look like a follower.

I could tell something was wrong with Geffel when she came back onstage after the intermission at Merkin, but I thought it might be temporary—I *hoped* it would be—until I saw her at The Kitchen several weeks later. That's when she went all the way off the cliff, musically speaking. That was such a disaster that I *had* to write about that. So I did, and the piece was published right away in the *SoHo News*—on the front cover, as everybody knows, under the famous headline, "Sweet Smells Despoil The Kitchen."

[Geldman is prompted to elaborate on what he characterized as "wrong" with Geffel.]

I keep forgetting you weren't there for any of this. You missed a lot. But you can call yourself lucky for missing what I'm talking about now. Geffel came back after intermission [at Merkin Hall], and she wasn't her normal self. It had to be obvious to anyone who had ever seen her before. She was missing that gravely serious expression she had whenever I saw her perform. She was smiling and swaying her head back and forth in time as she played. She smiled so broadly at times that her teeth showed. It made me realize, I had never seen Adrianne Geffel's teeth.

The music was, above all, the sure sign that something was *off*. The first piece she played was a soft, slow ballad—lyrical and soothing. It reminded me somewhat of Debussy's lovely works for the piano—things like the first movement of the *Suite Bergamasque*, "Clair de lune," or "Reflets dans l'eau," in the way the music evoked the stillness of a peaceful body of water. It was stunning, like nothing I had ever heard Adrianne Geffel play. I was baffled and horrified. I thought to myself, *What's going on? How could she do this? What's wrong with this woman?*

She played only a couple more selections before ending the concert at Merkin, and they were very much in the same aesthetic vein of beautiful pieces that conjured the placid wonders of the natural world. At the conclusion, she played something companionable but slightly variant—a buoyant waltz with a catchy tune and a gentle beat. I'll never forget it.

[Geldman hums several bars of an attractive melody.]

See what I mean? It was mortifying! Gone was the explosive irrationality, the dizzying emotional intractability of the music Adrianne Geffel had always made before this. There was barely a hint of the radical qualities that made Adrianne Geffel's music what the listeners in the lofts and galleries and critics like me knew—and acclaimed—as Adrianne Geffel's music.

A critic must always give the artist the benefit of the doubt. With this in mind, I excused Geffel for what I could only hope was a freakish lapse. I ignored that part of the program in the review I handed in, and went to the next performance she gave, on the opening night of her run at The Kitchen, with an open mind, hoping to hear the Geffel I could recognize again.

The Kitchen was very well known by then as the premier venue of presentation for a heterodox school of music and performance art that was not really very well known. It was on Broome and Wooster [an intersection of streets in SoHo], and it was the "inside" place for creative outsiders like Adrianne Geffel, Peter

Greenaway, Pauline Oliveros, Rocco De Petro, and celebrity oglers from uptown who had never set foot in any other kind of kitchen. After The Kitchen became a success, The Living Room opened on Stanton Street. As best as I can recall, there was no venue called The Bathroom. CBGB's served the function.

Geffel played a residency of a week at The Kitchen—six nights, no show on Monday. She had become a subcultural phenomenon—the doyenne of downtown music, in a phrase. I coined that and used it in a number of my pieces on Geffel, but you should feel free to use it, too. Just credit me—no copyright notice necessary. I was in the front row at The Kitchen for Geffel's opening and came back, after a night to recover from the shock, and saw the last four shows. I could hardly believe what I heard. Geffel played beautifully. She opened the first night with a lilting tone poem that wafted through the air of The Kitchen like the mist rising from a pond, and every piece to follow was just as disappointing. The audience, all seasoned veterans of the experimental music scene, wriggled in their seats and exchanged furtive glances in distress. Adrianne Geffel had delivered us to musical hell.

With each successive night of her residency, the audience dwindled. The word had gotten out that Geffel, for whatever reason, was suddenly incapable of producing or unwilling to produce the wild and furious, hostile, inscrutable music that had made her that doyenne of downtown music. I took no pleasure in holding her accountable for this in the series of articles I wrote on the subject, and in the additional criticism I added to my original review of the Merkin Hall concert for inclusion in my book.

N. D. Nieve:

As I wrote in the *Village Voice*, Adrianne Geffel, at her best, forced us to face the worst within us. Her art was nothing less, but everything more, than emotional truth revealed behind the false front of musical notes. She created from the inside out, and then turned that outside-in. To experience her music was to see and feel, to taste and smell, the inner essence of humanity with the palpable tactility of organs bursting from a body viscerally ripped apart. From the small stage of The Kitchen on a week in January 1984, Geffel undid all the undoing she had done. All she could offer was the sound of the sight of a pretty young person, intact and brushed clean, with glowing skin and a sparkling smile that said, "Enjoy me, for I have nothing more to give than the glistening, vacuous treacheries of joy."

Ann Athema:

I brought Jeffy with me, and we went to see Geffel at The Kitchen. We were there on the third or fourth night. I always loved Geffel's music, you know that. I couldn't always quite process what she was doing. But I loved the fact that she was doing it. This show that week was like the Merkin concert—the second half—but even more so. It was so rich and sunny, I was melting in my seat. I remember thinking, "What on Earth would I do if Geffel ever asked me to make art for this kind of music?" My mind drifted off to concepts I could use—confetti and marzipan, a long, warm bath . . . I started to giggle, and Geffel heard me and picked up the giggle in the music, and Adry's piano and I kept giggling together. Jeffy whispered to me, "I didn't know Adry's music was so . . . enjoyable." I whispered back, "It wasn't."

It was shockingly beautiful—shocking for Geffel's music—but as true and honest and deep as anything she ever played, and far more moving. I reveled in it. I found it transporting. It gave me a feeling of pure bliss.

Dr. Emil Vanderlinde:

Although I was not treating Adrianne on an ongoing basis, I followed her career with acute interest through the media. I was well aware of the events you're asking about. Two of the research fellows working under my supervision at the institute were responsible for monitoring developments in Adrianne's case through media accounts. They prepared quarterly reports for my assessment and alerted me intermittently to circumstances of special note. The reviews and so forth pertaining to Adrianne's performance conduct in 1984 documented a significant departure from her historical pattern of practice. Music reviewers found her output in this period to be highly objectionable.

It was apparent that Adrianne was experiencing a level of emotional satisfaction or happiness that had not been manifest in her behavior prior to this. Strong feelings of pleasure were attenuated in the superficial amygdala, which we know to be important to the experience of joy in humans. In Adrianne's case of psychosynesthesia, feelings of this character would trigger neural input from the amygdala and the hippocampus to the auditory cortex, taking form as aural hallucinations of pleasing music. Adrianne channeled those hallucinations at the piano to produce enjoyable musical sounds which, in turn, triggered intense displeasure among reviewers.

[Vanderlinde is asked to address how certain listeners can hear pleasing sounds as unpleasing.]

The phenomenon is one of social science, not real science. Neuroscience can come into play, however. Social responses to sensory input become normalized in the brain over time. Hence, an intellectual response that is socially informed and consciously asserted can, with repeated experience, evolve into an unconscious reaction. We know this as "learning to like" something. One can also learn to dislike. The brain rewires itself in accord, and the pleasant sounds that once stimulated the superficial amygdala register as unpleasantness in the lateral basal amygdala. Excuse me, but I can't tell if you're listening to me. Are you falling asleep?

[Vanderlinde is answered in the affirmative.]

Harvé Mendelman:

We had good money invested in the concert at Merkin Hall. Four hundred bucks, the venue charged us for recording off the soundboard. Top dollar. First class. High fidelity, stereo. Dolby sound. The tape they supplied us was releasable quality, technically. Musically, that was a different story.

I'm a market*eur*—you understand. I have good ears, and I know how to use them. I'm not saying I've got million-dollar ears. But they're half-million-dollar ears, maybe seven-hundred-fifty-, eight-hundred-thou ears. And when I use my ears, I use my brains. I listen to the people working for me. And I listen to the experts—the critics and the writers. Don't forget, our line of product is an upscale line. As I've explained to you, I call it our *avant*-line. I have to use my brains to be a market*eur* for our market. "Upscale" is what "avant" means, in another language. I'm almost sure of that.

[Mendelman calls through the door of his office.] Bethany—look up the word "avant" for me, will you? It's not English.

I wasn't able to attend the Merkin concert in person, by the way. I had a dinner engagement. I left that recording in the hands of my good friend Biran Zervakis. You must know from the live-in-concert album, *The Merkin Concert*, we released the entire first half of the program—three selections, which Adry named for us later.

[Mendelman again calls through the door of his office.] Bethany—bring in a copy of *The Merkin Concert* album for the oral-history man here, would you please? *Thank you!*

[Mendelman's assistant, Bethany Reyes-Edelstein, enters with a copy of the album and a slip of note paper. Mendelman hands the album to the interviewer, reads the note, crumbles it, and discards it.]

My friend Biran was producer, and he made the recommendation to shelve the second part for reasons of quality. He had my complete confidence, and I understood his reasoning when Adry gave her concerts at The Kitchen, and the reviews came in. Adry had taken an unfortunate turn and was making a completely different kind of music now.

I started to worry. The professor at the New School for Social Research who consulted for us [Dr. Stewart Rauschmittel] invited Adry to play for his students. He gave a lecture on Adry's music, followed by a performance. Called me afterward and told me the class was a disaster. The students were totally confused. Adry's music had nothing to do with anything he taught in his lecture. Told me, "Mr. Mendelman, you're in terrible trouble—she humiliated me in front of my students. I don't know what's gotten into that woman, but she's not the same anymore. If she keeps this up, she'll be the laughingstock of the avant-garde. She'll ruin her career and take Infini Records down with her." He used more impressive words. But that's the essence of it.

Dr. Stewart Rauschmittel, Ph.D.:

No, that [account, read to Rauschmittel] fails to do full justice to the debacle Adrianne Geffel incited in my classroom. I provided a foundational deconstruction of Geffel's aesthetic, interrogating the elemental paralogic and absonant discord that inform the art, but rarely misinforms it and certainly would never lie to its face. Geffel proceeded to present a program of indefensibly lyrical irrelevance. She nearly lulled the class into a state of blissful catatonia with her lilting melodies and luxurious harmonies. I could only think she must be joking, though I saw no humor in a display of such unremitting cheeriness.

Harvé Mendelman:

She threw us for a loop or two. Had to do something. Being a market*eur*, I knew I would have to market*eur* my way through this. Decided it was time to get Adry back into the recording studio and show the world she was still the same deeply serious and hard-to-listen-to Adry Geffel. Just then, she phoned me herself to propose a new recording project. I said, "Great, Adry—that's my girl! Let's set up a meeting with Biran, and you can tell us all about it."

She said, "I want to tell you *right now*."

I said, "I love that enthusiasm! Keep that. Bring it with you when we meet with Biran."

And she just launched into her pitch. Said she wanted to do a follow-up to the *Oh, Negative* album. That was her third record, live in the basement of the Judson Church. Nice seller for us, a critical sensation—fantastically challenging and unpleasant. Opened with "Gunpowder and Blush," closed with "Gutter Tumbleweed." I can't even listen to most of it. Classic Geffel! She said she already talked to the Judson Church people, and they were on board for recording there on their little Steinway baby grand. No audience this time, just her at the piano. The cost to bring in recording gear and the engineer wouldn't be cheap, but it was worth it to me to have some viable Geffel product to market.

I gave her the go-ahead and told her to fill Biran in on the details. She started to laugh. I laughed back, to be friendly. She hung up.

I don't know what kind of research you do for oral history, but if you read the police reports, you know how that went. Adry never told Biran anything about the recording plans. He got wind of it and showed up at the church on the day of the recording. Adry was already downstairs, playing. She had half the record in the can. Adry's girlfriend was planted in front of the door to the church with a team of lesbians to keep Biran out. Biran claimed that he only punched in self-defense—who knows?

Adry brought the tape in to play for me the next day. Biran was still in the hospital. My secretary, Karen, got the tape spooled up and ready to play. Adry said, "Remember—I see this as a companion to *Oh, Negative*, an answer to it. It will be called *Oh, Positive*, because the music is all very positive."

Karen pressed PLAY. I took a deep breath, closed my eyes, and as I listened, the music conjured mental images of a sun-drenched beach. Waves rolled slowly in and out as barefoot children frolicked in the sand. I ordered Karen to pause the tape. I said, "Adry, Adry . . . tell me, is the entire album like this?"

She beamed and said, "You bet!" She gave me some double-talk about some selections being in different keys and having various harmonic concepts—whatever. I looked her straight in the eye, and I said, "Adry, I'm sorry, but I can't release this, for your sake and mine. The critics would tear you apart, and you'd turn off the audience that you, we, have been working so hard for so long to build. This would do more damage to you and us than I can allow. Take some time off. Go away. Clear your head. Take a balloon ride and paint happy faces in the clouds. Get this out of your system. And come back when you're your old self again.

"After you do that—if you do that—call me. But if you don't or you can't do that, I'm sorry, we can't work together."

CHAPTER 8

The Devil and the Mailman

(1984–1985)

Biran Zervakis:

My Adry—my Adry . . . She was always my Adry—always and ever in my heart, and not only there. On paper, too—on every one of the albums I produced for marketing in her name and the copyright registrations for the music, and, since then over the years, all the legal papers, back and forth . . . The very name of the publishing company I formed and incorporated in the State of New York was there in print, right there in the fine print, for all to see if you look for it. I called it My Adry's Music, Inc. So, you can see that even in that dark, dark time when Adry and I were physically separated and she was away from me, across town to that dismal locale on Ninth Avenue, and not just physically—though ours was a relationship, if that word could be used to describe the indescribable what-it-was between us, that should never and shouldn't ever be thought of in terms of the merely physical—she was still My Adry, right there in the very name of the publishing company.

[Zervakis is prompted to explain why he sees this period as "dark."]

My God . . . my heart had fallen into darkness, longing for my Adry. And our home—the residence we had together, until we were no longer together, physically or otherwise, was quite literally dark. I kept the lights off in her room—the room where my Adry used to be, when I was home—to save money on electricity. Keep in mind, I was forced to carry the full burden of maintaining the apartment now. From the beginning, I had always handled the payment of all the bills, to spare Adry from worrying about such matters. I personally paid a full thirty percent of the costs of rent and utilities, including phone and cable, out of my own funds, filling in the rest by drawing on Adry's income from the performances, recordings, and publishing I was overseeing. After she left—I should say, after she was taken away from me—I paid the full sum of the costs of all the apartment expenses, which I was able to do successfully by continuing to draw from Adry's earnings for as long as possible, until she noticed.

[Zervakis is asked to verify the interviewer's understanding that Zervakis, as sole owner of My Adry Music, Inc., received fifty percent of the revenue from Geffel's publishing and, in addition, a manager's commission of twenty percent on Geffel's share, as district court filings indicate.]

Pardon me, did you say "court filings"?

[Zervakis is answered in the affirmative.]

You're a historian—you should know better than to believe what goes on in court. People will say anything under oath. Let's stay on topic, shall we? It was a dark, very dark, dark time in Adry's career. You must know that, since you're obviously so adept at *reading* things. Have you not read the media accounts of the downturn in Adry's music? She was on the verge of being dropped from Infini Records. I'll have you know, as a matter of fact, she was eventually [dropped], through no fault of mine, I'll have you know.

My dear friend Harvé Mendelman was stuck with the tapes Adry manipulated him into allowing her to record at the Judson Church. The music was unreleasable, unless Infini Records suddenly decided to go into the business of producing soundtracks for nature documentaries, and I refer not to the exciting kind about tsunamis and plants that eat human flesh. I refer to the kind about families of bunny rabbits and colorfully winged birds gliding off into the sunset. Harvé was going to hit me up for the costs of the remote recording in the church, and even after deducting those expenses from Adry's account, applied to future earnings, the prospect of those earnings diminishing in the imminent future was deeply disconcerting to me, as it would be to anyone whose financial well-being was dependent upon Adry and who truly cared about her and wished to maintain that well-being.

Nightline was in the process of producing a whole segment on the burgeoning downtown arts scene—"Weird Wonders of the New World of Music." They heard all about Adry and wanted to feature her. I was working directly with one of Ted Koppel's personal assistants. It was practically a lock. My contact—Ted's own assistant, one of the top ones—went to see Adry at The Kitchen, and that was the end of that. I called her office the next day, and then every day for several days after that, and when I finally reached her, she said, "Oh, I'm so sorry, but that isn't quite what we're looking for." I got the message—all of a sudden, Adry Geffel wasn't weird enough.

Something had to be done, and someone had to do it. If someone didn't do it, it would probably never get done.

Karen Gigliardi:

He called Mr. Mendelman, and I patched him in right away—Biran. I didn't make him wait, like Mr. Mendelman liked for me to make people wait, so it would look like he was always too busy to talk. I could tell this was real important. "Put me through to Harvé," Biran said in that cute little squeaky voice he had.

I could only hear Mr. Mendelman's side of the conversation. He didn't like the speaker phone—all those buttons! "Yeah, yeah—you don't have to tell me . . ." It went like that, but with curse words. "Okay—I'll tell Karen to get right on it."

He slammed down the phone and called me into his office. "Karen!" he said. "Set up a meeting with Biran and me. Soon as possible!" I got to work and arranged a meeting for the two of them for that same afternoon. Things were happening so fast!

I took notes at the meeting, like I always did. I don't have the steno pad anymore. Mr. Mendelman taught me, "Throw away the notes." He didn't like a paper record of the business happenings where people might find them some day. But I remember that [meeting]. Mr. Mendelman was all upset over the music Adry Geffel was giving him, which he didn't approve of one bit. He was ranting and raving to Biran—"What does she think she's doing? I can't release that . . . *stuff*." He used another word—you can use your imagination. "What's gotten into that girl of yours?"

Mr. Mendelman was beside himself because he thought Adry's music had gotten so nice. This made no sense to me. But I was used to that in my job. It was a learning experience. I remember writing down "lollipops and roses," because Mr. Mendelman said that about Adry's music. That stuck with me because my mother always, always sang that song—"roses and lollipops, lollipops and roses . . ." That's all I know of the song. I never connected that with Adry Geffel before. Biran started trying to explain that Adry was happy about something that he didn't seem to like at all, and that was why her music was so happy.

I said to myself, just being sarcastic to myself, "Oh, so, make the girl *unhappy*!" But I really said it out loud, without realizing I was talking.

Biran turned to me and stared at me for, it felt like forever. "Karen," he said, "that's what I call strategic thinking. Write that down. Now we have a workable plan."

Harvé Mendelman:

My friend Biran Zervakis tell you anything about the emergency meeting I called?

[Mendelman is answered in the affirmative.]

He came soon as I called him. Didn't even take the time to buy flowers for Karen. [Mendelman once again attempts to laugh.]

We brainstormed a strategy, and I gave Biran and Karen their marching orders. Told them, we are Infini Records—we are experiment*eurs*. We will experiment our way out of the Geffel problem, as I called it.

First thing we did, my concept—I tapped the expertise in experimentation I had developed to put Infini on the map of the new-music world when we launched our first line of product, *The Infini Archive of Anomalies of Musique Mechanique*. I told Karen, "Send the tapes Geffel made at the Judson Church to our mastering lab, and tell them to use their imagination. Run them backwards, quarter-speed. Cut them into pieces, throw the pieces in a hat, put it on their head, dance the Cossack Dance, and splice the pieces back together. Go to town with the tapes—any town they want! Go to a town in another state, in a whole other part of the country. Go to Florida with them, in their minds."

The lab got the message, sent back a master no one would ever be able to recognize or listen to. I had no idea what they did to those tapes, and I didn't want to know, till I got the bill and asked for an itemized breakdown of the job.

I gave Karen instructions to call the professor at the New

School for Social Research we used—you know who I mean, Professor You-Know-His-Name, very famous—and have him write up some liner notes and give us a good title for the record. Karen asked me for the master tape to send him. I explained to her, "Karen, you should know by now, we need the master to press the record. He doesn't need to hear the music just to write about it."

I knew now we'd have a product we could release. Biran wanted a producer credit, and that was only fair, in consideration of the fact that he'd be getting a good percentage of the revenue. We had a meeting to map out the release plans with Biran, and Karen piped up, "What about Adry? Do you want me to cc her on anything?"

Biran told her, "Let's just make it a big surprise."

Karen said, "Well, she's not going be very happy about this."

Biran gave her a little pinch on the cheek and said, "Thank you."

Dr. Stewart A. Rauschmittel, Ph.D.:

I was commissioned by the Infini Record Company to compose an essay of postulations regarding a project of aggressively processed and edited electronic music by Adrianne Geffel. In concept, it was a radical departure for her and conceptually fascinating to me. The company provided me with a lay person's description of the project, in memorandum, which referenced the work by the title *Oh, Positive*, presumably in irony. You would know the project by the title I gave it, *Oh, No*, which is self-evidently a fitting rhetorical parallel to the music, as I understood it in concept from the memorandum. I refer you to my essay, which has been published not only as an eight-page booklet accompanying the album, but later in expanded form in my monograph, *Spinning Discourses: Toward a Theory of the Rubric of Disequilibrium in Avant-Garde Text and Pretext*, revised second edition. The latter would be the more viable source for your reference, the album having been withdrawn from distribution over a dispute with Geffel's representatives or estate. I was not a party to that. I have been told the album has become a collector's item. I wish now that I had a copy of it myself. It would be stimulating to read my essay again, and it could be interesting to hear that music.

Ann Athema:

I went over to Geffel and Barb's place fairly often—probably more often than I went when it was Jeffy's place, because it didn't use to be so sanitary. I had to meet Geffel once because it was the first of the month and she had to pay the rent, and she misplaced the slip of paper Jeffy had written his Carmine Trembler signature on for Geffel to copy. Jeffy whipped off a great new one for her. The date for this was the first—June or July, an insufferably hot summer day in New York City—and the day of the week was a Wednesday, I'm certain of that because the *Village Voice* was published on Wednesdays, though you could get it after midnight on Tuesday night while you were out, if you wanted. I picked up a copy that morning on my way to Ninth Avenue. Geffel and I liked to look through the S&M personals in the back, for laughs, and pretend we were going to call Mistress Igor or Mel Torment for a nice lashing and golden shower. We sat at the island Barb built in the kitchen and flipped through the *Voice* together. Barb wasn't there that day. She probably had a building job. I admired Barb enormously for her ability to do things I had no patience for, such as work.

We're flipping through the *Voice*—flip, flip . . . flipping through the pages . . . there's Michael Musto, there's the Feiffer ballet-dancer cartoon, flip, flip . . . [Athema mimes turning pages in a newspaper.] And there's a big photo of Geffel—looks like a record-company handout—with a full-page article. Geffel slaps her hand down on the page. We both start reading, and it's a review by N. D. Nieve of a new Adrianne Geffel album, complete with a reproduction of the cover in the corner.

I say, "Hey, Geffel—congratulations! Is this the Judson record?"

Geffel yanks the paper away from me and reads the piece to herself, pacing around the apartment and humming a strange tune. She stops reading and drops down on the floor. There was a chair a few feet away, but she plops straight down onto the floor and sits there, holding the paper in her hand. She's still humming this weird, atonal tune, and then she starts singing to herself, putting words to the tune: "How the fuck . . . could they do this to me? How the fuck . . . could they do this to me? How the fuck . . . could they do this to me?"

Karen Gigliardi:

Mr. Mendelman told me to make an exception to his rule about phone calls and, if Adry Geffel called, "Don't make her hold on the line and wait till I pick up. Tell her I'm not in at all, and just take a message." I did that before, with a couple of the vendors and some of his girlfriends and his wife, so I knew how to do that and not be too bossy about it, so people wouldn't get mad at me. Mr. Mendelman said I missed my calling—I should have been an actress. He was such a *charmer*. I bet he's the same way with his new secretary—excuse me, I mean his new *executive assistant*. Nobody's a secretary anymore. I wonder if they still even have a Secretary's Day. That was a nice thing.

[Gigliardi is pressed to continue her recollections.]

Oh, forgive me—I didn't realize you're not interested in my opinion on things. I suppose you only want *opinions* from Biran and Mr. Mendelman and the other *men* with the fancy titles.

[Gigliardi is given an apology and encouraged to speak freely.]

Thank you very much.

One of my responsibilities was to keep a clipping file of all the articles about the company printed in the newspaper and the magazines, and catalog them. I was much more than a secretary, it shows you there. In the time you're asking me about, Biran told me to buy an extra copy of one article and take it to the poster shop on Lexington Avenue and have it framed for Adry, just log the cost on her account, and give the nice, framed review to him so he could present it to Adry.

[Gigliardi is asked if she is referring to the review of *Oh, No* published in the *Village Voice*.]

Yes. It was the only time I was ever asked to do that, have a review framed. I told Biran, "I know what's going on here, you know. I know what you're doing."

He said, "Why, Karen—it was your idea, don't forget."

I said, "Well, I don't have to like it."

He said, "The important thing is that Adry doesn't like it. That's the best thing for her, trust me. It's for the good of the whole company, and you're an important part of that." He sounded very serious, even with that silly little voice of his.

Adry started calling Mr. Mendelman that day. I did what I was supposed to and told her, "I'm sorry, Adry, but Mr. Mendelman isn't in at the moment. I'll make sure he gets your message." She kept calling back, three or four times a day. After a couple of days of this, I came in to work in the morning, and Adry was there already, waiting outside the door to the office. She was sort of pacing and humming something a little scary-sounding.

I unlocked the door. I had the keys, because Mr. Mendelman didn't exactly keep business hours—he had an *artistic temperament* and things to do outside the office with the accountants and the lawyers. I started to tell Adry that I wasn't sure when Mr. Mendelman would be in, and if she would like to leave him a message . . . She shot me down real fast and said, "Karen, I'm going to stay right here." She paced around by my desk, humming something very peculiar.

I went into Mr. Mendelman's office, like I had to pull some papers, and used his phone. I called Mr. Mendelman, and he said, "Well, I'm not coming in there. Call Biran. Thank you, Karen." He was always such a *gentleman*.

So I called Biran, and he said, "Wonderful! I'll be right there." I came back out of Mr. Mendelman's office, carrying some papers I pulled out of his file cabinet for show, and sat back down at my desk and did some work. Biran walked in a couple of hours later, holding the review I got framed for him and acting like he just happened to be in our building and thought he'd stop by to chat.

He said, "Why, Adry! What a surprise! I'm so *happy* to see you. How are you? Are you happy, too?"

Adry marched straight toward him, and Biran handed her the framed review—"Look—I have a present for you!"

Adry took it, didn't even look at—she just stared at Biran—and let it drop out of her hands. It fell onto the floor and smashed while she just stared Biran in the eyes. She said—I'm not sure how to describe this—she was talking . . . she wasn't yelling at him, but she sounded almost like she was singing. She said, "Goodbye, Brian." She called him Brian—weird. "Goodbye. Do . . . you . . . fucking . . . hear . . . me?"

Biran said, "I hear you very clearly, Adry, and I *love* the way you sound. That's my Adry!"

And Adry left the office, crushing the glass on the floor as she walked out.

Barbara Lucher:

I don't want to talk about the bullshit we had to deal with. Just look it up. Don't you have a *library card* in that purse of yours?

[Lucher is reminded that the historical record on the relevant issues is incomplete, and that the term for what the interviewer carries is a shoulder bag.]

So, what do you want to know about? You want to hear all about the *money trouble* and *legal trouble* and *real-estate trouble* we had that we never should have had? You want to know how it *felt* to be fucked in our fucking asses by every ass-fucking fuck-ass in New York?

[Lucher is answered in the affirmative.]

I really hate this.

[Lucher stands up, sits back down, and wipes her face with the tail of her shirt.]

Alright. Okay. And I'm sorry for insulting your accessories. I know what a goddamn shoulder bag is. Ask me something specific.

[Lucher is asked to elaborate on what she means by "money trouble."]

That's not very specific. But okay. We had a damn sweet setup—great apartment . . . useless neighborhood, you know, but great apartment when I got done with it. I was working steady. Good thing, because Adry's income was drying up. Biran—know what, I'm not going to call him that anymore. His fucking name was Brian. Adry told me. *Brian* had finagled control of Adry's business income, and was draining whatever she had accumulated from her record sales and concerts—I don't know how much, Adry never got legitimate financial statements—so he could pay his own rent and buy cases of imported dead-baby blood to drink. We were living on the money I was making from building jobs after a while. No complaints. I was doing alright.

Ann and Jeffy helped Adry find a lawyer to take on Brian, but that wasn't paying off yet. It was costing us—quite a bit, out of what I was bringing in. But we were holding our own, and then Adry was home alone one morning, while I was working. There was a knock on our door, and it was some guy from the New York City government, like a process server for the city, hand-delivering a warrant for Barbara Lucher. He handed it to Adry. She read the envelope and told the guy that's not her name, and he ran out like the rat he was.

The second I walked in the door, she filled me in and handed me the envelope. I opened it up—I wanted to just light a burner on our stove and torch it, but Adry talked me into reading it first, and then I could torch it. I could not be-fucking believe my fucking eyes. It's a nasty legally notice from the New York Department of Buildings for violations of the building code in a job I did, subcontracting for the contractor Philip Glass hooked me up with. Fat wad of fines, thousands of dollars. And I'm prohibited from doing any further construction work in the five boroughs of New York until the matter is resolved to the satisfaction of the department. *And* the company that subcontracted me has been notified, so there goes all my future work with my main client down the toilet, and it's one toilet not even Philip Glass could fix.

How much do you know about interior construction? Scratch the question. I'll explain.

The New York City building code required that the vertical studs in load-bearing walls be spaced at a distance of twenty-four inches. The job I was doing was a kitchen renovation. I broke down a wall to extend the kitchen by three feet. So I had to build a replacement wall. I spaced the studs at sixteen inches, which is the way walls used to be built, and the way I was taught in Pennsylvania. It's not New York City code—only better.

The city also specified that the lumber in interior construction had to be number-two pine. Today, it's all metal, fireproof. But in the Eighties, the requirement was number-two pine. For this job, I happened to use number-one pine, which is planed without knots and stronger, but costs more usually, except I got a deal at Prince Street Lumber, so I used the superior lumber—superior, but not New York City code.

And the city required that wall surfaces be made of three-eighths-inch gypsum sheathing—sheetrock. I used five-eighths-inch, and not only that, I used "blue" grade, which is waterproof. Stronger wall, less susceptible to mold in the damp environment of a kitchen—better, but not city code.

It took weeks for us to figure out what was going on, and by then we were flat-on-our-asses broke. Somebody in music circles must have mentioned to Harvé Mendelman at some point that Philip Glass helped get me work. Mendelman or Zervakis—

which one, who knows? Who cares? One of them, conniving to make trouble for me—and that means trouble for Adry—strong-arms or scams or bribes some pussy in the Department of Buildings to look up the permits to see where I'm working, and they do a spot inspection after I leave one day, scouring the site to find anything they can use against me. Nasty, sneaky, completely unethical but weirdly legal, and head-fuckingly effective. A few phone calls and a couple hundred bucks folded in a newspaper, and I am totally fucking fucked.

Ray Octavio:

I did my business clean. Never a problem with the government, no trouble with the unions and the mafia. I was clean like my own mother.

The lady got in some trouble. [Octavio refers to Barbara Lucher.] I told her, "No—this, I cannot have." I pay taxes. People give me tips for all the work I do here. They show me their appreciation like that. My wife enjoys the cable television. She has family out of the country, and she likes to call them long distance. She has the numbers she has to have to do that. I don't want trouble with anybody. We're clean. You have trouble, you take care of it. It has nothing to do with me. I don't need the government to come into my house and see things.

I told the lady, I have no problem with you. You and your friend, live the way you want. [Octavio refers to Lucher and Geffel.] My people are Catholic—we have the nuns. But now, you cannot work for me now. I don't want trouble. I have a clean business.

[Octavio points to the interviewer's recorder and makes a gesture indicating that he would like it turned off. While the recorder is paused, Octavio makes a hand gesture to indicate that he would like a cash payment. The interviewer demurs, and Octavio departs.]

Jeffrey Knudsen:

I was still getting some mail at Ninth Avenue. I didn't do a change of an official address with the Post Office, because I never *had* an official address in my name. Every couple of weeks, Ann would bring home any mail I got, when she saw Adry. One night I came home from work, and Ann left a little pile of mail for me, and she put a note next to it that said, "Carmine—for you! Took care of Ray." The second part of that meant that Ann took care of tipping Ray, the super at the building. The mailman always gave FedEx packages, certified mail, registered mail—anything that required a signature—gave it to Ray, and he signed his name, and you just picked it up from him and gave him a little something for the service. There was a certified letter addressed to Carmine Trembler. I had a beer. Then I poured myself a shot of Jameson. And I had another beer. And I opened the letter.

It was a summons to appear at housing court to verify my identity as legal signatory to the lease to the Ninth Avenue apartment—not my identity, Carmine Trembler's identity. I sat and read that, and I thought, I guess this means it's time for another shot of Jameson.

Karen Gigliardi:

My mother always said, "the Devil and the mailman!" If she ever had her own sitcom, that would be her big catchphrase. They'd have it on coffee mugs and underpants. I never asked her what it meant, because the way she said it, you were supposed to know. But when I grew up and got this job, I understood—you can do your darnedest to keep a secret, but nothing gets past the Devil and the mailman! Don't you forget, the mail is how I found out that Adry and Biran were together, when I saw that the two of them had the same mailing address. *Who knew about that?* The Devil and the mailman!

It was the day Adry called me to tell me to mail her things to a new address that I realized, *Oh . . . well, so much for Adry and Biran!* I kept sending the business papers to Biran at the old address on 3rd Street, because he was the one who handled all the business at their household. But I sent the fan mail and unimportant things like that to Adry at her new address, which was 114 Ninth Avenue. I remember it because I had to type it a number of times in the letters I did for Biran that he sent out at the time of the "Geffel problem," as Mr. Mendelman called it. Biran had the lawyers look into various things involving Adry, and they found out that her apartment wasn't really her apartment—it was in somebody else's name. Biran got all revved up about that and wrote a number of letters to the city that I typed up and mailed for him.

Jeffrey Knudsen:

I had enough drink in me to call my uncle. He was a tough guy—scared the crap out of me, to be honest, but he got me the place on Ninth Avenue as a favor to my mom, so I had to deal with him. He was in the butcher's union, I told you, and looked like a bull himself, actually. His face was even bright red, like a bull in a cartoon. I read the letter to him over the phone. I could hear him breathing heavy and could almost see the puffs of smoke coming out of his ears. I read the whole letter, and he didn't say anything for a long time. Finally, he said, "You sound tired. Or drunk. Are you drunk?"

I said, "No, no—no, I'm just tired. I'm *exhausted*. Working too hard—you know what that's like."

He said, "Working too hard, at the MTA? Doing paperwork?"

I said, "I guess so."

He said, "Jeff, I know you appreciate the value of having such an apartment for the kind of rent you pay, and you enjoy living there. You *do* enjoy *living there*, don't you?"

I said, "Yesss . . . I *do*." I couldn't tell if he knew from my mom that I had moved out and was living with Ann now or he was just being a hardass or I was paranoid.

He said, "Then you know as a professional in the area of municipal paperwork that there's one way and only one way to satisfy the requirements of the Department of Housing in this situation, and that is to deliver Carmine Trembler. That would be very difficult. I'm not saying I am privy to knowledge of the whereabouts of Carmine Trembler or even if he's still alive or not. I'm not saying. I'm just saying your only recourse is to deliver such a person. Good luck with that—and, you understand, of course, I and the Amalgamated Meat Cutters cannot be associated with this. Goodbye, Jeff. Don't work too hard."

Ann was sitting by me this whole time. I told her what he said, and she said, "I like that uncle of yours. Hand me the phone."

Ann Athema:

I called Armutt Canterell. I said, "Armutt! How is the Medici of modern music, the guru of the galleries, the Rooster of Wooster Street? Drop everything you're doing! I'm working on a new project, and I need a very special collaborator. Only you can help me."

I told him I had an inspiration to create the most exciting conceptual art of our time. It was so conceptual I couldn't explain it in words. It transcended language. It defied all modes of representation. I would allow him to experience it before anyone else, as soon as it was ready. But first I needed his help. The work required the involvement of a collaborator named Carmine Trembler. Armutt said, "Tell me, who is that?"

I said, "No, Armutt—*you* tell *me*! All I need from you is to find an unknown artist in your armada of unknown talents, and change the person's name to Carmine Trembler, like you changed my name to Ann Athema and gave new names to Irma la Douche and Van Guardrail. It needs to be done as officially as possible by next week. I'm so excited!"

He tried to slow me down. He said he didn't *get* the name Carmine Trembler.

I said, "Oh, Armutt . . . *please*—don't be such a philistine. No one is supposed to 'get' it. That's the point. *Armutt, Armutt* . . ." I told him to meet me at Dimicci's on Monday afternoon, with Carmine Trembler in hand, and I hung up.

On Monday afternoon, Geffel and Barb, Jeffy and I, went to Dimicci's, and Armutt strolls in with a guy—middle-aged, scrawny, stringy gray hair hanging down to his shoulders, he's wearing a long-sleeve shirt buttoned to the collar, and it's the heat of summer—and Armutt introduces us. "Ann, Adrianne, everyone—this is Carmine. Carmine—this is Ann and Adrianne and everyone."

Geffel gives him the onceover, and Armutt launches into the guy's biography. He was an associate of Harry Partch's who worked with Partch on the instruments Partch constructed out of found objects to play the rogue music he composed with microtonal scales of his own creation. He got to know Partch when they were both residents of a hostel for homeless men, and they later lived together as a couple under the interstate underpass in Sausalito. One of the instruments he and Partch concocted was a xylophone made with liquor bottles of various shapes and sizes reclaimed from the trash bins of Northern California barrooms. "To resonate properly," the guy said, "the bottles needed to have no remaining alcohol. I assisted Harry at that and other duties." Geffel started to hum one of her odd, atonal tunes, and Barb reached over to her and massaged her neck.

Barb asked the guy some questions about instrument construction, and he seemed to know what he was talking about. He came from Indiana, he said—"the Indianapolis Tremblers." Everyone nodded and sipped their espresso.

Armutt asked me to tell him about the exciting new project I needed Carmine for, and I gave him the "shsssh" sign. "Armutt, *please* . . . an explanation would only demean my concept. I can only say this much: You're familiar with the Warholian notion of 'business art,' of course. This goes even further than Warhol. You could call it 'law art,' if you insisted on giving it a name. But I insist you not. My canvas is the abstract principle of justice. Let me see the papers you've gotten for him."

I looked over the flimsy ID materials Armutt pulled together in a few days' time—a Polaroid of Armutt and our man, signed "To Armutt from Carmine Trembler," and a one-day pass to the Museum of Modern Art. I said, "Not terrible. This is more than I have in the name of Ann Athema." Jeffy opened an envelope he brought, and laid out an old lease and utility bills in the name of Carmine Trembler. Geffel flipped through everything and said, "Koshka, I'm not sure *art* is the word for what you're doing here."

The court date came up a few weeks later. We all chipped in to buy the old guy a suit of passably semi-decent clothes. Jeffy's uncle recommended a lawyer who knew his way around the courtroom and appeared familiar, even somewhat friendly, with the judge.

We all sat in the back. That Biran was there, on the other side—we kept our distance. I looked over at him for a second, and he waved at me like we were old friends who just so happened to be at the same movie. We had to strain to hear what was going on as the two lawyers took turns addressing the judge, almost whispering. The judge asked our guy a few questions, and he came across as confused and, perhaps, more than a bit nuts. The judge gave a cursory look at the paperwork, shook his head, signed a document, and pounded his gavel. Geffel and Barb would have their apartment back.

The plan we made was for the new Carmine Trembler to stay on Ninth Avenue with Geffel and Barb for a week or so, sleeping on the couch, and then quietly return to his previous life. Unfortunately, he had nothing to return to and no reason whatsoever to vacate an attractive and clean, low-rent apartment that the New York City housing court had declared to be rightfully his. In a matter of weeks, he drove Geffel and Barb out of their own home—littering the place with scraps of half-eaten food he scrounged from the fridge, yapping incessantly at full voice to no one in particular, peeing on the floor of the bathroom . . . Geffel and Barb were broke and ill-prepared to pay the deposit on a new apartment, and moved in temporarily with Jeffy and me on Ludlow Street. We knew the old guy wouldn't be able to keep up with the rent on Ninth Avenue unless someone came along to cover it for him, which is exactly what Biran did. Biran had instigated the trouble with the apartment, and he finished the job.

The Ludlow Street place was too small for four—four people

plus the baby grand piano we couldn't leave on Ninth Avenue. The piano became our all-purpose living surface. We laid out dinnerware on it, and it became our dining-room table. We set up a typewriter and papers on it, and it became our desk. At night, Geffel and Barb cuddled up on a cushion under it, and it became a canopy bed. Geffel even used it as an actual piano, playing music that seemed to get weirder and darker by the day. Hearing myself describe this, it sounds like kooky bohemian fun, like the setup for an NYU student art film. But it was stressful and unsustainable. We were four adults hiding inside a carboard box. I was picking fights with Jeffy. He was working late every night, to keep away. And Barb and Adry were miserable. Barb simply said so—"This sucks." And Adry let it out in her music, which was getting unbearable.

The three of us, all but Jeffy, were there together on the night Biran called. Adry was playing piano, and Barb was lying underneath it to rest. I picked up the phone. He said, "Good evening, Biran Zervakis here." I didn't reply.

He said, "And this must be Barbara Lucher."

I said, "*Must* it?" I covered the receiver with my hand and mouthed to Adry that it was Biran. She kept playing, but louder and harder.

He said, "Aaah . . . I can hear Adry playing her music. She sounds just like the Adry I know and love. Put her on the phone."

I said, "No."

He said, "Then take this message. Tell Adry I would like

to help her bring in some money. I suspect she could *use* a little money. Tell her to put the date September 8 on her calendar. She will be giving her premiere performance at Weill Recital Hall, in Carnegie Hall." This was in the middle of August—I remember because of the suffocating heat. That put the concert at two or three weeks away.

Biran said, "I can tell from the music she's making right now that Adry is her old self again."

I said, "Yes, this is Barb Lucher. So fuck you, you fucking fuck-fuck!" And I hung up.

Barb crawled out from under the piano while Adry kept playing, she looked up at me and said, "Nicely done."

Adry continued playing, and the music got stranger and stranger.

Karen Gigliardi:

Biran called for Mr. Mendelman. I put him on hold and had a piece of Russell Stover's—the nougat with the crumbly, crackly tiny pieces of filberts are my *favorite*—and patched him in. Mr. Mendelman came out from his office with his chest puffed out and his hands on his hips like Ethel Merman, and made a big announcement, "The Geffel problem, as I call it, is over. Karen—bring in our copywriter! We have an advertisement to write."

I dialed up Mr. Mendelman's nephew, Scott, the boy who did all the writing and promotion for us, and set up that appointment.

Scott went off and made a very professional advertisement and a matching poster, and Mr. Mendelman paid for everything. It was a big to-do! I asked Mr. Mendelman, "Mr. Mendelman, will you be requiring my services at the concert?"

He was very kind. He said, "Don't worry, Karen—you don't have to go."

I told him, "Oh, no, Mr. Mendelman! I'd very much like to go to this! I've never been to Carnegie Hall before." Mr. Mendelman explained to me that this particular concert was in an area of Carnegie Hall they called Weill Recital Hall. I got his meaning on the night of the concert, when I had to go in a different entrance and up an elevator, but it didn't matter to me one bit. I still got to say that I had been to Carnegie Hall! That's more than Adrianne got to say.

Carolyn Geffel:

Yes, Greg and I knew all about the big night at Carnegie Hall. Nina Oberheimer heard an announcement for it on the classical-music station in Philadelphia. Greg and I don't get that station, I don't think. I'd have to find out where it is on the dial and try to tune it in. We thought about going in to New York for that. We were way overdue for a return journey to the Big Apple, and it would have been lovely to be in touch with our Adry once again. I tried to get tickets, but couldn't reach Adry on the phone to ask her to take care of it. There was an answering machine with a man's voice at the number we had for her. I told Greg, and he said, "Hang up—that can't be where Adry lives." He could be so nasty sometimes.

So, we didn't go, and it was just as well, in terms of seeing Adry.

Jon Geldman:

I'm sure you've read my essay about that evening at Weill Recital Hall. I don't have much to add to what I've written on the subject and already expanded upon for re-publication in my book. Obviously, the event was a great disappointment to those of us who were at Weill Hall that night. However Adry Geffel may have felt about it is another matter.

Ann Athema:

Geffel left the house early that day—I imagined, to get her hair done, test out the piano in the hall and survey the space, and primp before the show. Jeffy and I went later, just about an hour before showtime. Barb, I presumed, would be with Geffel. We got to Carnegie Hall and found our way to Weill. I left Jeffy in the lobby and talked my way backstage, to see if Geffel needed anything. I asked a stagehand to point me to the artist's dressing room and knocked on the door. No answer, so I opened up the door: No Adry. I went back to the same stagehand and asked if there was another dressing room where the performer might be, and was told no, Adry was supposed to be in that empty room.

I scouted out the whole area backstage, to make sure Adry hadn't been bonked by an errant sandbag or fallen down a trapdoor. No Adry and no sandbags or trapdoors. I checked my watch, and it was 7:58, two minutes till curtain. Biran burst backstage and started darting around, hunting for Adry. He gave me a stare, and I just shook my head.

Jeffy was still waiting for me in the lobby. I ran up to him, and he said, "What's the story?"

I said, "I haven't a clue."

Jeffy said, "Maybe she got delayed on the subway. You can't rely on the MTA. Let's take our seats."

We sat there, squirming and periodically scanning the stage area for signs of movement. At eight-twenty, Biran came onstage and said, "Ladies and gentlemen, we're very sorry, but Adrianne Geffel will not be appearing tonight." He kept talking, but I didn't listen. I said to Jeffy, "That Geffel—she's fucking Biran over! She's a pisser, that Geffel! Let's go home—she's probably waiting for us."

We went straight to our apartment. When I got to the door, I knocked the corny old "shave and a haircut" knock, but nobody knocked back "two bits!" Jeffy unlocked the door. I walked in slowly and noticed that the door to the clothes closet was wide open. I looked in it and saw that all the clothes Adry had hung there were gone.

I sat down on the piano bench, my head fell onto the top of the piano, and my arms crashed down on the keyboard. A sound very much like the sound of Geffel's music rang through the air, and I never saw Adry Geffel again.

EPILOGUE

The first time Adrianne Geffel went missing, as a girl of nine, a couple of able troopers from the Pennsylvania State Police soon found her, asleep in the back of a truck. The next time, when Geffel was twenty-six and nationally renowned as a pianist and composer, a couple of State Police officers, no matter how able, would not be sufficient. The search for Adrianne Geffel has gone on for decades now, with little to show in the way of solid information. Most of the information we have on Geffel's status since her disappearance is *un*solid: fluid—slippery and ever shifting; gaseous—thin and ethereal; and everything else that *un*solidness means or suggests as a value fungible as any term of analogical forced poeticism.

This much we know from the historical record since Geffel's disappearance:

Ann Athema, working under her legal name, Valerie Koshka,

in collaboration with her first husband Jeffrey Knudsen, arranged for Geffel's previously unheard music to be released on an independent label they formed for the purpose, Adriatic Records, its name a play on the notion that the music came from "the Adry attic." (Infini Records' suit against the label, contending that it unfairly infringed on Infini's brand association with the Adriatic region because Infini had sold recordings by the Albania Symphonette and the Slovenia Navy Chorus, is unsettled at this writing.) The first project of the new label was Geffel's album, *Oh, Positive*, in the form Geffel intended, with all the original recordings, unedited and undoctored. Athema (Koshka) and Knudsen restored the overtly positive titles Geffel had written for the tracks, such as "April Face" and "Lullaby for Barb." (See the Discography in the back of this book for a full rundown of Geffel's known recorded output.)

In addition, the new label released a collection of home recordings Ann Athema found on cassettes Geffel had been storing in her piano bench. Athema was unaware of the existence of the tapes until piano movers arrived at her apartment unexpectedly, under telephone orders from Barbara Lucher, to ship the instrument to Beethoven Pianos in Yorkville, and Lucher opened the lid of the bench for the first time. (According to Athema, Lucher was the beneficiary of the sale, which transpired shortly after Geffel disappeared and immediately before Lucher left the country; in all likelihood, the sale funded Lucher's travel and, Athema surmises, aided Geffel as well.) Athema and Knudsen named the album for one of the song titles Geffel has penciled onto the cassette J card, "Yummy Sounds." The release comprises four complete pieces, including yet another tune in tribute to Lucher, "If She Were a Carpenter," as well as a series of joyful fragments that Geffel recorded under the umbrella title "Chew Toys."

The critical response to these albums in the classical and "new music" press was tepid to harsh. Even so, the records changed the conversation about Geffel and re-positioned her as a multipurpose symbol of strong emotions of more than one kind of musical expression. She was now recognized as an artist with a unique ability to give voice to human passions of varied colors, from stark black to warm pastels. The later albums never sold in pop-hit numbers; still, the general public's lack of familiarity with the music in its particulars only enhanced its utility as a locus of cultural discourse and a fulcrum of debate.

The mystery of Geffel's disappearance factored significantly in her rise from provincial urban glory as the "doyenne of downtown music" to mainstream cult status—a kind of fame for being unfamous, an ephemeral figure whose absence imparted an aura of cryptic martyrly untouchability. Norman Mailer tackled this mode of thinking and, after making the tackle, fell on top of it and passed out, in his booklet-length "essay" on Geffel, *Arrivederci, Adrianne.*

One can only presume Geffel herself would have been gratified to see the release of her later work, music evocative of what may have been the happiest time in her life. Then again, she may well have been even happier the day after she disappeared and happier still the day after that, and so forth. We know nothing for certain about Geffel's life—or if, in fact, she has been alive—since the evening of the aborted concert at Weill Recital Hall. In the absence of knowledge and certainty, theories and fantasies about Adrianne Geffel have flourished. Many of the most credible, the somewhat plausible, and the wholly unlikely postulations about Geffel's possible fate were dramatized in the TBS infotainment special, *Whatever Happened to Adrianne Geffel: How Good Is Your Guess?*

After her disappearance, journalists started digging into Adrianne Geffel's history, and news of her neurological condition and her role in the development of the Sony Walkman surfaced. In an article published in the annual audio-equipment insert to *Rolling Stone*, Sony engineer Kazuhiro Takashima, father of Geffel's Juilliard classmate Sue Takashima, told the story of his finding the inspiration for the Walkman in the cassette-recorder-and-headphone setup he saw Geffel wearing. The piece, by electronics journalist Robert Heffer, went on to describe Geffel as "the girl genius" whose "mix-and-match audio accessorizing" made her "arguably the mother of what could be called 'personal entertainment'" or "at very least the pretty thing who caught the father's eye." Although Sony contested the account and demanded a retraction (which it received, as a major source of hi-fi advertising revenue), the tale became part of the lore of the young tech industry, and fed the theory that led off the TBS special.

In this hypothesis, Adrianne Geffel attracted the attention of developers at Samsung, then an under-achieving player in a fledgling Korean electronics industry emulating the Japanese model.

Samsung slyly, quietly lured Geffel to South Korea and set her up in secluded luxury, hoping she would generate a bounty of concepts for unimaginable wonders of electronic gadgetry. In the TBS take of this possibility, Geffel (portrayed by Phoebe Cates), accompanied by Barbara Lucher (Alyssa Milano), stumbles onto a country school for girls during a morning walk and joins the children in song. Geffel bonds with the girls and, taking advantage of the tech facilities at Samsung, develops a whole new genre of cheery, electronically processed music that comes to be known as K-pop.

In another hypothesis, Geffel moved halfway across the world in the opposite direction, to the Middle East. Struck by accounts of Geffel's habit of wearing headscarves in public (to shield her ears from ambient music), a few writers wondered if Geffel might have relocated to an Islamic community, where she could be physically shrouded inconspicuously. Implausible at first glance, if only for the challenges life under orthodox Islam could pose for Geffel and Lucher's relationship, this notion gains some credibility upon close examination of the careers of two Muslim women notable in the field of electronic dance music. Priscilla Bakalian, a DJ from Lebanon, and Magda El Bayoumi, an EDM producer of Egyptian/Polish descent, have both talked in interviews about having been influenced by similar encounters with a mysterious woman in a Hijab (El Bayoumi used the phrase "Shabh in a Hijab," using an Arabic word for phantom) whom they heard on the street, making eerie sounds as she passed by. "The woman I saw was an American," said El Bayoumi. "She made strange music. Who else could she be?"

Rumors and speculation about Adrianne Geffel lace through the recent histories of every genre of music that accommodates extremes. A sampling:

- Adrianne Geffel and Barbara Lucher moved to the West and took up farming. Settling in Boise, Idaho, Lucher worked behind the scenes for a construction co-op for women in agriculture, and Geffel put together a noise band called Magic Sword. To protect her identity, Geffel performed masked and cloaked, under an obtuse stage name, and persuaded her bandmates to do the same. The group made a dark music with an Eighties feeling sometimes described as "neo-Geffel" or "would-be Geffel." Might the "would-be" be a "could-be"?
- Geffel, presumably accompanied by Lucher, again, relocated to Sweden. She continued making music in the joyous, tuneful mode of her later work in New York, got a sex change, and became Max Martin.
- Geffel, with or without Lucher, found a flat in London and hatched a way to record and release music with no public profile, using digital technology. She created a virtual band of digital avatars and named it Monkeyz in homage to the Sixties made-for-TV group the Monkees. Unfortunately, a pair of British men, Damon Albarn and Jamie Hewlett, stole the idea and used it for a virtual band they call Gorillaz.
- Geffel left New York, with Lucher, to live quietly in rural

Warren County in northwest New Jersey. At the recommendation of Laurie Anderson, they leased a patch of land outside the village of Blairstown, where Anderson and her husband Lou Reed kept a country hideaway. Geffel continued making music, in secret, with Anderson and their neighbor Keith Jarrett, while Lucher worked as a foreman for a local builder, Hajdu Construction, a company founded by my uncle Louis. This theory has gained considerable currency since word of my work on this book surfaced in publishing circles. I am in no position to confirm or deny this proposition, though I wish it were true. That would be cool.

- Geffel and Lucher moved back to the area of western Pennsylvania where they had been born and raised. They set up housekeeping just a few miles from Geffel's parents' propane business on Route 6 in Venango County. Geffel enjoyed making music at home, in private, and Lucher made a woodworking shop to sell craft furniture by mail order. No one from New York looked for them there, and no one in the county recognized them anymore. This is among the most feasible of theories about Geffel's whereabouts, if also the most boring.
- And then there are those who believe—or, in romantic morbidity, wish to believe—Geffel died, either on the night she was supposed to play at Weill Hall or at some point over the ensuing years. Images of Geffel as a spectral presence appear in songs from artists as notable as the art-

pop singer-songwriter Jill Sobule, who wrote a cheekily mournful tribute to Geffel, "Adry in a Dream":

I think I met Adry
Once in a dream
I asked her to sing with me
She said oh no, oh no
In my part of heaven, we don't sing
We scream

As we know from Anastasia Romanov, Jimmy Hoffa, D. B. Cooper, and other cases throughout history, tales of mysterious disappearance can spark dubious visions of reappearance. Innumerable Romanov cultists thought they saw Anastasia for decades after she vanished, and, for all we know, some may really have seen her. Over the years since Adrianne Geffel disappeared, a small but slow-growing group of Geffel enthusiasts have reported and compared notes on "Adry sightings." The earliest I know of were shared on the now-dead early AOL listserv, wheresadry@aol.com, which predates the period of my scholarship on Geffel and would be a lot of trouble for me to find at this point. Inevitably, Twitter quickly became the nexus of information from and for people around the world who believe they might, could, or should have spotted Geffel somewhere. The hashtag #isawadry served this purpose for a time but stirred some confusion among admirers of the Palestinian-Scots poet Isa Wadry. In time, #isawadry2 became the go-to source on "Adry sightings," and, indeed, was the place where I first learned about some of the theories on Geffel's whereabouts outlined above. (See also: #isawadryintheday, which deals with the time of Geffel's activities in New York, and #isawadryinthenight, which is in the vein of fan fantasy.)

Of all the witnesses to Adrianne Geffel's life I interviewed for this book, one, Barbara Lucher, no doubt holds the secret of Geffel's fate. Lucher, in response to my request for her participation in this project, agreed to take part only on the condition that she would not answer any questions about anything after the events at Weill Hall. But I never promised not to *ask*.

At the end of the allocated time in the last of my sessions with Lucher, I asked, "Could you tell me if Adry Geffel is alive and well?"

Lucher said, "What the fuck do you fucking think?" and prompted me to answer her.

DISCOGRAPHY

The Music of Adrianne Geffel

CONCERT RECORDINGS

Biran Zervakis Presents Adrianne Geffel
(Infini Records, 1980. Recorded live at the Jervic Loft.)

1. Black Frost
2. February Face
3. Not Sure I Like This
4. Bosenbuttons
5. Where I Live (w/"spoken language" by Darius Epstein)
6. Variations and Fugue in E-Flat major and Seven Other Keys

So Far, SoHo

(Infini Records, 1980. Recorded live at the Jervic Loft.)

1. Fuck Cunt!
2. It's Different for Me
3. Grand Street Grand
4. Flammable Material (Duet with Bobby Akbar-Aleem)
5. Now/Not Now
6. Burnt Host (for Milijenko)

Oh, Negative

(Infini Records, 1981. Recorded live in the gym at Judson Church.)

1. Gunpowder and Blush
2. False Positive
3. Ann Anthem
4. On the Invention of the Filterless Percolator
5. Honeymoon in Marshalsea
6. Gutter Tumbleweed

The Merkin Concert

(Infini Records, 1983. Recorded live at Merkin Concert Hall.)

1. Waking Up in a House Fire
2. Poodles of Blood
3. No Standing Any Time

STUDIO ALBUMS

Chords and Baffling

(Infini Records, 1982.)

1. Pane Relief
2. Baby Grave
3. Second Honeymoon in Marshalsea
4. Secret Exit
5. Terrible Likeness
6. Hell's Kitchenette

Oh, No

(Infini Records, 1984. Original tracks recorded in the gym at Judson Church, edited and processed by Infini Musique Laboratories.)

1. Oh-One
2. Oh-Two
3. Oh-Three
4. Oh-Four
5. Oh-Five

Oh, Positive

(Adriatic Records, 1986. Recorded in the gym at Judson Church.)

1. Sweet Somethings
2. April Face

3. The Third Sock
4. This Shall Not Pass
5. Lullaby for Barb

(Compositions published by Geffel's Own Music, Inc.)

Yummy Sounds
(Adriatic Records, 1987. Collection of home-recorded music compiled by Ann Athema.)

1. Yummy Sounds
2. Djuna and the Moon-a
3. If She Were a Carpenter
4. Elegy for the El
5. Chew Toys (fragments)

(Compositions published by Geffel's Own Music, Inc.)

OTHER

Lofty Ideas: The Smithsonian Anthology of SoHo Music of the 1970s, 1980s, and Other Periods

(Smithsonian Institution, 1994.)

Various artists. Includes one track, "February Face," from Adrianne Geffel.

Unless otherwise noted, all compositions published by My Adry's Music, Inc.